AROUND THE YUKON STOVE

A Collection of Alaskan Tales

By

One of the Gang

Mary J. Barry

M J P BARRY
323 West Harvard Avenue
Anchorage, Alaska 99501

FOR: MELVIN, RONALD, RICHARD, AND JOHN

Names and incidents that appear in these sketches are fictional, unless indicated otherwise, and are not based on any person, living or dead.

M J P BARRY
323 West Harvard Avenue
Anchorage, Alaska 99501.

Printed in the United States of America.

ISBN: 0-9617009-1-2

First Edition, 1988

INTRODUCTION

Somewhere between the Alaskan megapolises of Anchorage and Fairbanks, but far beyond the back of the Bush, so far back that they haven't even heard of Anchorage's greatest tourist attraction, the Bird House, lives a band of sturdy Alaskan sourdoughs of various ages and two sexes, in a community known as Malamute Heights. Some have been in the Land of the Midnight Ice Fog since the Great Gold Rush, while others are more recent, but just as enthusiastic, Last Frontier stampeders.

Although they are so independent they won't even apply for Food Stamps or the Alaska Permanent Fund Dividend, they occasionally feel the call of human companionship, which causes them (in winter) to dig their way out of their half-buried cabins or (in summer) to brave mosquitoes, gnats, and no-see-ums in order to gather at the cozy log cabin of the oldest old-timer of them all, Sourdough Jack, and sit around the glowing Yukon stove as they amuse and amaze each other with stories from past and present.

One of the group, in the great tradition of Boccaccio and Chaucer (Fred B. and Elmer C., journalists of Lost Gulch, Texas) finally took ballpoint pen in hand and recorded some of these unusual reminiscences, with the view of entertaining and edifying both cheechakos and sourdoughs.

Now, it has been set into print, for all the world to read and to learn about America's last frontier, the great state of ALASKA!

Note from the Publisher

While critiquing Northern literature (a popular pastime hereabouts), the opinion arises frequently that the Alaskan Mystique, as exemplified by Jack London and Robert Service, is passe in the modern Forty-Ninth State, as exemplified by Anchorage. Some even deny the existence of an earlier Alaskan Mystique, believing it to be just a romantic illusion of the fore-mentioned authors and their followers.

It was, therefore, with some astonishment that we received the manuscript containing these conversations, which prove that the Alaskan Mystique was not only alive but rampant in the little-known Interior Alaskan settlement of Malamute Heights.

We remarked to the writer, whose name shall be withheld for h(is)(er)* personal protection because of h(is)(er) close association with those whose tales are told here, that a couple of the stories sounded vaguely familiar, as though we might have previously heard something similar. S(he)* replied that Sourdough Jack, the protagonist of several tales, had been in the North so long that some of his exploits had become part of popular lore, carried throughout the Northland by means of the Snowshoe Wireless and the Mukluk Telegraph. That explanation was good enough for us!

---

* Pronominal devices to further obscure the identity of the writer.

Sourdough Jack

Sophia Anna List

Igor Bivor

Lackoff Forsyte

Captain Stormdecker

Phoebe MacDusaldorf

Ophelia Bumbleforth

Blodge Bumbleforth

Justa Succor

By Richard Barry

The Author

AROUND THE YUKON STOVE

CONTENTS

PART ONE

THE COUNTRY

The Great Alaskan Bear Tale

One evening, without knocking or any further ado, as Social Club speech makers are wont to say, several of Sourdough Jack's neighbors burst into his cabin and slammed the door.

"What's the commotion?" drawled Jack, shifting his Old Norse snoose about in his mouth.

Breathlessly, they exclaimed, "Wolves! We were halfway over here, when a pack of bloodthirsty, ravenous wolves spotted us and pursued us, their mouths agape, their teeth flashing, and their saliva dripping!"

"Is that all?" Sourdough Jack opened the door, to face the snarling, snapping pack, and aimed a shot of liquified snoose at the leader. As the odoriferous projectile struck among them, the pack took off, whimpering and whining.

Jack returned to his still-agitated audience. "That reminds me of the closest call I ever had!"

They were all agog to know what could be worse than a pack of murderous wolves, so they gathered around the Yukon stove as Jack crammed another half-pound of Old Norse in his cheek pouches and commenced to speak.

"It was back in the days when I was prospecting on the island of Kodiak, when nuggets were big and the bears were even bigger. I was just in the midst of panning a promising stream when the largest Kodiak bear I'd ever seen ambled up.

"He laid back his ears and acted as though the stream and all the fish in it was his personal property and his alone. Meanwhile, I backed slowly towards a large tree about thirty yards away. As he crouched to charge, I shinnied up the tree, wearing off a foot-wide streak of bark in the process. Up in the branches, I looked down on him, kinda sneering, because I knew he was too heavy to climb a tree.

"Well, he stood up and scratched as high as he could go. Then, he snarled and stamped about. After that, he laid down at the roots and took a nap. By this time, I was getting a little tired of this game, and a little hungry besides, but I wasn't about to take any chances climbing down among a ton of fur, claws, and teeth.

"Finally, old bruin woke up, stretched a bit, and ambled off. 'Aha!' I thought, 'He's given up. I'll get down and get out of here!'

"Holy moldy cranberries, was I fooled! Before I could move a leg, the bear appeared again, followed by three beavers. He stretched up, reaching for me expectantly, while the beavers commenced to cut down the tree."

Jack stood up, shot some snoose into the Yukon stove, and the dancing red flames turned blue as they sought to devour this latest fuel offering.

"What happened then?" "Were you hurt?" "How did you get away?" came the excited exclamations from all sides.

"It's such a long story, I'll have to tell you the rest some other time," answered Jack. "My jaws are tired."

Although Jack's friends begged for the rest of the story many times, Jack never did feel that he had enough leisure to tell it. They think, however, that they know the answer. When that beast got within a nose's breadth of Sourdough Jack's Old Norse-soaked hide, the greatest bear on earth completely lost his composure, his bravado, and his appetite, leaving our hero intact to tell the tale.

A Survival Tale

The Malamute Heights residents were getting jumpy. One of their younger and greener members, Lackoff Forsyte, had wandered off into the woods on an afternoon hike and hadn't turned up, over a week later. When a person lives out in the brush beyond the toolies, one day is a lot like another, so the tendency is not to notice the time passing. But after several days of not seeing their young friend showing up at their doors with cups to borrow sugar or flour, or whistling loud, atonal melodies as he stirred his fish head stew and porcupine marinade, or the slamming of his outhouse door at 5:30 a.m., the neighbors began to get worried. They gathered at the Yukon stove and allowed that maybe they should organize a searching party, if Forsyte didn't show up soon. After much discussion, they decided that if their friend failed to turn up in a month, they would draw up a plan for such a search.

At that moment, a large helicopter suddenly appeared over their heads and settled to earth in front of Sourdough Jack's cabin, scattering leaves, dust, and malamutes.

Out came Forsyte, surrounded by several efficient-looking forest rangers, state troopers, federal game officers, and other authoritative figures, the likes of which hadn't appeared in this neck of the elderberry patch in a long time.

They handed Forsyte several thick books of regulations, lectured him sternly, then mounted the helicopter and rotored off into the blue yonder.

"What happened to you?" "Who were they?" "What is this all about?" queried the astonished group, question tumbling over question.

"To start at the beginning," commenced Forsyte, after requesting coffee, doughnuts, cookies, blueberry tarts, and homemade ice cream from his friends, to fortify himself for the tale, "I set out on an afternoon stroll and soon found myself hopelessly lost in an almost impenetrable forest. I wandered about for days, with no clue as to my destination, at the mercy of the elements. I heard no sound other than the sounds of the deep woods. I saw no human nor even the footprint of another person. No one, I was sure, but wild beasts of the timberland had ever trod there before. I despaired of ever being found. Finally, I came to the conclusion that only by using woodcraft would I survive.

"I thought back over all the Grizzly Adams and Davy Crockett shows that I had seen. Bits and pieces of wood lore came back to me. I took limber roots and devised a snare for rabbits. I heaped up leaves under a spruce tree, and built a shelter there with fallen branches. I gathered dry, dead spruce twigs and cottony plant fibers, and made a revolving drill to twirl and heat up sufficiently to start a fire.

"I completed all of my labors, took a rabbit from my snare, cleaned it, and put it on a stick to roast over my crackling fire, while I lounged on my leafy bed, when suddenly I heard a roaring sound from the sky, and I was surrounded by officials of the government. I was bewildered by the almost unfamiliar sound of voices, but finally I began to make sense out of the hubbub. They were informing me that fires were allowed only in authorized campgrounds, and asking me whether I had a subsistence permit to catch rabbits or a license to cut trees. I was too astonished to answer. Finally, they doused my fire, confiscated my rabbit and leaves as evidence, wrote an environmental report, fined me, and brought me back here. I have been warned never to enter the woods again!"

"Never? Not even for a weekend?"

"No, never ever at all!"

"Well, Lackoff, welcome home! We're almost glad to see you're back!"

The Year of the Big Freeze

One January evening, Sourdough Jack's cabin was crammed with one of the largest assemblages of Malamute Heights residents seen in a Sik-sik-puk's age (marmot's age, to you cheechakos). The tiny community in the outpost of Alaskan wilderness had endured below zero temperatures and howling winds for a week, and everyone had come down with cabin fever -- everybody but Jack, that is. He had prepared for the ordeal of winter early in the fall, gathering blueberries, currants, crowberries, raspberries, salmonberries, rhubarb, low- and high-bush cranberries, and watermelon berries, smashing them, and brewing the seething, bubbling mass until it reached the ultimate percentage of alcohol, then corking it in sundry explosion-proof bottles.

Conversation immediately turned to that reliable topical standby, the weather.

"Wow, is it cold! exclaimed one of the more recent arrivals to the backwoods. "Every time I breathe out, I look like Mt. Katmai having a smoker's fit."

"I haven't been able to move my furniture for a week," lamented Ophelia Bumbleforth. "It's all frozen down to the cabin floor!"

"I tried to wash my long-handled underwear the other day, and the arms and legs broke off!" remarked Lackoff Forsyte.

"How cold did you say it was?" inquired Sourdough Jack.

"Fifty below!" three voices shouted at once.

"Fifty below?" snorted Jack. "You call that cold? Back in the days of the Great Gold Rush, we'd have considered that a mild winter's day!"

"Yes, but what about the chill factor? That brings it down to 75 below!"

"Holy hooting horned owls, it was so cold during the Gold Rush that we didn't even bother with cheechako chill factors! The coldest winter I remember was so cold that there was no chill factor. The air was so heavy that it squashed the wind right down to earth and held it there, tight. Not a molecule could move. Not a sound could travel anywhere. Everything was quiet and still, like the beginning of time."

"How cold was it, exactly?" asked Igor Bivor, one eyebrow raised in disbelief.

"No one will ever know just how cold it was, because this chill came on so sudden that every thermometer and barometer in Circle City landed on its lowest point at once, with a thud, sending a shock wave that vibrated through the town. We all thought at first it was an earthquake!

"Then, most of the trees in the area exploded! The little bit of moisture that remained in them expanded so fast that it blew the bark and wood to smithereens. We couldn't hear the reports, of course, but those of us who were outside had to duck the flying branches.

"We ran into our cabins and fired up our Yukon stoves to weather this out. One fellow stopped to spit on the way, and we had to break him loose from the long icicle that stretched from his mouth to the ground.

"Well, this cold continued for way too long. I don't know how long, because nothing mechanical, not even the clocks, would move. We piled on every bit of long wool underwear, pants, shirts, vests, jackets, hats, gloves, scarves, furs, and blankets we had in our houses.

"All the lakes froze clean down to bottom, and kept on freezing even more until the ice was so compressed down in the ground that the deepest layers commenced to heat up. They built up such a head of steam that they created the hot springs you find in different parts of Alaska to this day -- I suppose you've heard of Circle Hot Springs and Manley Hot Springs, not to mention those on the Seward Peninsula? Why else do you suppose there would be hot springs in a cold place like Alaska?"

Jack shivered at the remembrance, and swigged a shot of his anti-freeze.

"I suppose that was the worst weather you ever encountered in Alaska?"

"It was **bad**, but I won't say it was the worst. That was the year of the Great Thaw!"

"I've never heard about that! What happened that made it so terrible?"

"You'll have to wait another day," Jack said. "It's too hard on my constitution to tell of such trying times twice in one day!"

He poured each of them a tiny glass of his remarkable brew, and they all leaned back in their chairs, basking in the glow from the Yukon stove.

The Year of the Great Thaw

Malamute Heights' cold spell was long over by the time Sourdough Jack got around to telling his neighbors about the year of the Great Thaw and its extraordinary consequences.

"You know how hot it gets in the Interior of Alaska during the summer?" he asked. "The sun shines twenty-four hours a day. There's no sea breezes to cool things down, but generally something holds it back from climbing over 100 degrees 'fair and hot!'

"Well, the year of the Great Thaw, something went wrong with the mechanism. The sun kept shining, the temperature kept climbing, and nothing shut it off! Pretty soon, it hit 115 degrees, and the tundra started turning brown and curling up.

"After that, that stuff they now call permafrost, but which I called darn fool ice that made it hard for me to mine, began melting. Pretty soon, the whole land was a soggy mess, with water seeping to the surface and flooding everything until it evaporated enough to make room for the next batch.

"Then, the land began to sink. I kept moving my cabin to higher ground, but even the hills began to lose altitude as their foundations washed away.

"Now began what at first was a nightmare for me. I awoke one hot night, to hear terrifying roars and screeches, like nothing I'd ever heard before.

"I looked outside for the source of this commotion, but all I saw was large bubbles rising from the depths of the water, which used to be tundra around me, and heading for the surface. Otherwise, there was nothing moving for miles, except the usual birds and mosquitoes.

"As I watched, a bubble reached the surface and cracked open. Out of it rushed the frightful roars that had roused me from my slumber.

"It took me awhile to figure out the origins of these sounds. During my days of mining, I had often struck large bones underground, the remains of long-dead mastodons, saber-toothed cats, and other prehistoric beasts. The incredible truth dawned upon me -- I was hearing their long-refrigerated roars as these animals struggled to escape from whatever frightful freezing catastrophe had befallen them and wiped them out, so long in the past. The screams, frozen at the site, had been released thousands of years later, during the thawing of the permafrost. I was hearing cries actually made millenniums earlier!

"I hastened to dash off a letter to my friends at the Smithsonian, who had always expressed interest in the relics I found. They were greatly excited, and immediately came north--a motley group of paleontologists, anthropologists, and even linguists. I asked why they needed linguists. They said, 'Since you were so helpful, you can come along with us and find out.'

"We all got aboard a paddle-wheel steamer, as that was the only way to get around Alaska during the year of the Great Thaw, with half the North under water.

"We headed off in the direction of the Bering Straits, they consulted their maps and notes, and we dropped anchor at their chosen spot.

"There they sat, happy as razor clams at high tide, notebooks and Edison wax cylinder recording phonographs at hand, preserving the babble of sounds rising from the water. Many of these sounded so much like human voices that I could hardly believe what I heard. Finally, I asked them what they thought they were.

"One of them explained, 'It has long been our theory that man came to American from Asia via the Bering Straits. Thanks to your awareness and the happy circumstances of the Great Thaw, we are hearing voices from some of those early migrants. From the collection we make, we will organize and analyze the sentences and phrases and finally get some on-the-scene accounts from these very first pioneers of America!'

"Thus, the question of how man got to North American was resolved at last. If you don't believe me, open this jar that I have carried with me for the last eighty years. Listen carefully as you do it, as you will never hear it again!"

Jack dusted off a gallon jar on his shelf and carried it over to his visitors. It contained some dingy water that resembled the average type one finds in an Alaskan swamp. In the center hovered a large bubble.

One of his guests cautiously unscrewed the rusted jar lid. The bubble rushed to the surface, and all present heard a voice speak in some strange, unrecognizable language. Then, the last shred of bubble disintegrated and the room was again still, as everyone stared in awe at Jack and the jar of liquid.

Even the most skeptical persons in the crowd stood silent. They filed out quietly and scattered to their various cabins, filled with emotion at actually hearing a voice from out of the lost corridors across the Bering Straits.

A New Winter Sport

Even though no roads have yet been carved through the forests and swamps that separate the small settlement of our intrepid pioneers and the busy arteries of vehicular commerce known as the Glenn and Parks highways, there are an amazing number of decrepid automobiles around the remote and rustic cabins of Malamute heights. I mean, what respectable Alaskan homestead doesn't have at least a half-dozen automotive hulks rusting in its yard?

The ex-college student, Igor Bivor, stumbled over one such object decorating his front yard as he sauntered out of his cabin early one morning. As he rubbed his shin tenderly, he looked over the cause of his accident, and thought he recognized a Volkswagen Beetle.

"I had one of these once in California, and it was fun tooling along with it on the freeway, holding up all the traffic. Wouldn't it be great to fix this one and drive it about again?" he mused.

He set to work with a Will, also a Mike and a Bob, because these were the names of his neighbors. Between the four of them, it wasn't any time at all when a bright shiny Volkswagen emerged from the three-inch shell of rust that had completely enshrouded it. The auto had an eclectic, even raffish, appearance, with sundry parts gleaned from the remains of Buicks, Fords, Chevrolets, and Dodges used to replace various missing portions.

One problem still remained. No roads led in, out, or about the tiny Last Frontier enclave. Where to go, how to give Volksy a real try-out?

"No worry," said Igor. "Winter will come."

His friends were puzzled at this, until he pointed out a cleared-out meandering route up the mountain behind Malamute Heights, that had been scoured smooth by a long-gone glacier. "I'll use that nature-made road this winter for some auto-slaloming."

Well, no one knew what auto-slaloming was, either, until Igor Bivor drew them a picture illustrating this new sport, which should, now that it is finally revealed to the rest of the world, be a smash on the winter fun scene.

Through Dark of Night

Mail day is exciting at Malamute Heights. Once or twice a year, a plane flies over and drops a bag of mail to the waiting townspeople below, who pounce upon it and eagerly scan its contents. Once in awhile, they get a genuine, first-class, personal letter, but most of the time, what they get is a notice from some publishing discount company, saying they could have maybe won ten million dollars if they'd only sent in their entry four months ago, before the deadline expired.

After one such mail drop, Justa Succor, an aspiring artist who had once sent in a request for information on an application she had found on a matchbook cover, came to the gathering at Sourdough Jack's to get the opinion of the group regarding an art and investment proposal she had received.

On parchment paper, embellished with a corporate coat of arms and gilded heading, was typed, neatly and certainly individually, these words:

Ms. *Justa Succor*
Star Route X
Malamute Heights, Alaska

Dear Ms. Succor:

Our sources indicate that you are a person of rare discrimination and impeccable taste. Therefore, we have chosen you to be one of the first to receive this unique opportunity to acquire a rare piece of art.

No doubt, Ms. Succor, you have heard the phrase, "Come up to see my etchings"? The etchings referred to were undoubtedly Rembrandts or Durers, completely out of financial reach for the average art lover. Now, at last, you too can become the proud owner of a genuine ENGRAVING!

These objets d'art have been carefully crafted by the finest artisans. An inspection with a magnifying glass will reveal work of such amazing detail and precision that it will take your breath away. The colors chosen are a restful gray and green. The paper is one of a kind -- especially made for these engravings only -- and contains REAL SILK THREADS!

Every loyal American will be thrilled to know that the subject of these exquisite engravings is a portrait of George Washington, FATHER OF OUR COUNTRY! As an added touch, each and every engraving is individually numbered and carries the personal signature of the _Secretary of the Treasury!_

And here is the best news of all! YOU can own this exclusive engraving (this year's edition has been strictly limited to ten trillion) for ONLY TEN DOLLARS! For an additional fifteen dollars, we will encase this art object in a pink poly frame that you would be proud to display on your wall!

One more word. Most collectors are concerned with investment opportunity, as well as beauty, in their acquisition of art. I can say with all sincerity that this piece of art is the ONLY one in the world that constantly depreciates in value. Therefore, I urge you to buy it _immediately_, DO NOT DELAY, as it will never again be worth as much!

Yours in art fellowship,

Marmaduke Q. Makeabuck
President, Kant Lose Investments

The group mulled over Justa's letter, trying to grasp the significance of it all. Then Sourdough Jack said, "There is a way this great offer can benefit everyone in our group."

He took his poker, opened the Yukon stove, and tossed in the letter. Everyone cheered as the flames brightened and cast a warm spell about the room for a minute or so, then they left for home to reread their own letters.

Spring: The Season for Plants and Grants

During an attack of whimsy last fall, Sophia Anna List wrote an application for a grant and sent it away to an office of the federal government, believing that they would derive a laugh or two from it and send it back to her. To her astonishment, her grant application was read, discussed, and approved.

Now, she told her friends at Malamute Heights, she faced a dilemma. Should she inform the government that it was all a joke, or should she go ahead with the project and perhaps earn everlasting, worldwide fame as the subject of one of Senator William Proxmire's Golden Fleece Awards?

The Malamute Heights residents read her application and opted for everlasting, worldwide fame for Sophia and her innovative spring project:

Applicant: Ms. Sophia Anna List, Malamute Heights, Alaska

Nature of Document: An application for government grant #129,377,966: Nature and Environment Research Project.

Specific Subject of Study: To document the unique characteristics attributed to the Easter Bunny.

GENERAL CATEGORIES OF INVESTIGATION:

1. Seasonal Appearance. Appears just once a year, invariably on a Sunday, but not the same Sunday every year. However, the Sunday on which it makes its appearance is always an Easter Sunday.

2. Reproduction. There is a problem of classification: Is it mammal, bird, reptile, or fish? It has fur and lays eggs. Sometimes the eggs are chocolate, other times they come out hard-boiled and decorated in exotic patterns. Sometimes they have the composition of jelly beans, and there are many sugar-coated varieties. The Easter Bunny generally deposits its eggs in baskets.

    Perhaps this mysterious creature is in the same family as the duck-billed platypus (a monotreme or egg-laying mammal).

3. Habitat. Den or hatching place has not been located. The subject is frequently seen hopping down a path called a Bunny Trail.

STUDY PROPOSAL:

The selected government agents will station themselves on the Bunny Trails, pen and notebook at hand, with cloth nets to painlessly capture any rabbit seen hippity-hopping along the trail with a basket hanging on its forearm.

PRACTICAL APPLICATION:

We believe that the Easter Bunny is a fertile subject for investigation and perhaps an answer to fluctuating egg supplies, if its production period could be extended beyond Easter Sunday.

Strange Encounter

"I'll bet you ran into some peculiar situations in the days before Alaska was mapped out and airplanes reached into the last hiding places," remarked Lackoff Forsyte to Sourdough Jack during one of the Malamute Heights meetings around the Yukon stove.

"Let me tell you! Things were different then. You never knew what lay around the next bend, and you couldn't count on anything being the same, one day to the next.

"Reminds me of the time I was out on the Alaska Peninsula tending my trapline. I had made the rounds and my dogs and I were mushing to our home cabin, hungry as wolverines. Although it was getting dusky, what with the early sunset and the tall trees along the way, we went at a good pace, because we'd been over that trail so many times we knew every bump and bend.

"All at once, my leader said, 'Worf?!' and disappeared before my eyes. The rest of the dogs dropped after him, followed by the sled and me. We found ourselves about eight feet down in a hole we'd never seen before, right splat in the middle of our trail. It was growing dark rapidly, but I'm a nosy type, so I groped my way around the hole. It was a large oval depression, about twenty feet long, with five smaller pits at one end. I was baffled as to its origin, until it came to me that it had the shape of a human foot. We had tumbled into the track of an Alaskan Bigfoot -- that mystical creature of the woods, well known to the Native inhabitants of the region!"

"Hold on there!" exclaimed Harry Happenstance. "I read about Bigfeet in Washington State and saw pictures of their tracks. Their feet are only about twice the size of ours."

"In Washington, yes! But in Alaska, everything's bigger, as you well know. Ask any Texan!" Jack looked a bit aggrieved at this questioning of his veracity.

"To get on! When I realized what we were in, I immediately wrestled my dogs and sled back up to the surface to get out of there before the maker of the track returned. Just as I got the harnesses straightened out and we were ready to mush on, we were overwhelmed by a pungent, peculiar odor. We looked up, to see a towering, hairy figure standing over us.

"Before I could yell to the dogs to get a move on, this creature reached down and scooped dogs, sled, and me into his gargantuan hands. Even the dogs were too scared to yip and I figured I'd seen the last of the dancing northern lights, the glowing Dipper, the steadfast North Star, the rugged face of Denali, the ....."

"Get on with the story, please!"

"Well, the giant looked about as puzzled by us as we were by him. He poked us about with his big thumb, then he slung us into a pouch hanging from his shoulders and strode off towards the mountains.

"With the big steps he took, it didn't take any time at all to be high above timberline, where the rocks were rugged and the air was thin. This didn't bother him at all, however. He jogged along, humming a bit as he went, while we bounced up and down in the pouch. As we traveled along, the air suddenly felt warmer. I thought this most odd, since we had reached a high altitude and had been going through snow all the way. Cautiously, I peeked out and saw that we were descending into the gaping maw of an active volcano. I became as worried as a bear in a taxidermist's shop and wanted to get out of there fast, but knew I wouldn't survive a leap onto the jagged rocks beneath me. Resigned to a fiery fate, I crouched down among my faithful dogs.

"Then the bouncing stopped and I felt myself being lowered carefully to the ground. The cloth walls were dropped and I and my dogs looked out at a broad plain inside the volcano. Warm, humid tendrils of steam drifted from scattered holes, but the rest of the land was crowded with lush fern-like trees, fruit-bearing shrubs, bushes bearing great, brilliant blossoms, the whole thing as riotously verdant as a jungle, and all brought about by the heat from the volcano.

"A group of furry giants stood around us, and it appeared that they were talking about us, although they communicated only in grunts.

"The Bigfeet kept us with them in the volcano for several weeks. I think they regarded us as pets. We weren't caged up or confined, but their hearing was so keen that we couldn't make a move without attracting their attention. Although we were treated well and I was dining on luscious fruits and tender, sweet vegetables, such as I hadn't tasted since leaving the South, I was getting awful lonesome for my own kind. Maybe they felt my unhappiness, as one day the Bigfoot that brought me there loaded the dogs, sled, and me back into his carrying bag and took off over the lip of the volcano and down to the valley below. There he left us, and we watched him vanish among the foothills.

"When my friends asked me where we had been, I just told them I'd decided to stay out on the trail, as I wanted to protect those creatures from the curious and from harm. After all, they had been kind enough to me.

"Ten years later, this region exploded and disintegrated, turned into an ashy desert by the eruption known as Katmai. I wondered if any of the creatures survived. Although people tell of Bigfoot traces to this day, no one has come up with the real thing. I myself went back a few years ago, but found nothing.

"If I hadn't kept this -- " (Jack rummaged around in one of his gunny sacks) "I wouldn't believe my own memories any more. I found this caught on a tree branch not far from where the Bigfoot dropped me off."

He pulled out of the sack a small bundle of tangled reddish hair too heavy for human hair and too long for any known animal. His friends looked it over and finally concluded that it had to come from something special, as it had no resemblance to anything that they had ever encountered.

Richard Barry

Sourdough Jack and the Iliamna Monster

Jack had held his audience entranced as he related his encounter with Alaska's Bigfoot. His listeners had barely recovered from their wonderment over the actual hair derived from the hide of a Bigfoot, when Sourdough Jack commenced to ramble and reminisce further.

"Those Bigfeet gave me some anxious moments, but nothing compared to my trip through Iliamna Lake with the Iliamna monster."

"What, may I ask, is an Iliamna monster?"

"You mean to say you haven't heard about the Iliamna monster? Some think he's a fish, others say he's a living prehistoric relic, and a few say he's hogwash! I don't know what he is, but he's gotta be the biggest water creature on earth!"

"Big as a whale?"

"Well, maybe not **that** big. Trouble is, he didn't give me time to measure him.

"It was while I was trapping on the Alaska Peninsula," Jack went on. "Iliamna Lake is awfully big and awfully deep. I had heard tales that some kind of creature that lived in those waters had actually grabbed animals that came to the edge of the lake and swallowed them. I was one of those who thought this was hokum, when I first heard it.

"Summer had come and I had gone down to the

lake to catch a mess of fish to dry and preserve to feed my team during the winter.

"I had just netted a big salmon, when the water appeared to boil before my eyes. Knowing of the temperamental volcanic nature of this region, I feared that a fissure was opening up beneath me. I stepped backwards, in time to see a huge gaping mouth, studded with sharp, gleaming teeth, emerge from the water and head straight for me, fast as a freight train. I had a glimpse of the biggest set of tonsils I'd ever encountered before everything went black.

"For a minute, I believed I had passed out. I couldn't see anything. I couldn't hear anything. The only sense still available to me was that of smell -- and my entire olfactory system was overcome by an incredibly strong fish odor.

"Then I began to see a bit of my surroundings. I was in a watery area, and small darting objects were giving off light. I scooped up a handful, and discerned that I was holding some small phosphorescent creatures. I suddenly realized my whereabouts and the danger of my position. I was standing smack dab in the giant stomach of the gigantic creature of the lake! The only thing that saved me from being dissolved by its stomach acid was the large quantity of water it had swallowed when it gulped me in -- and in just a matter of time, the water would be gone and I would be at the mercy of its digestive juices!"

Jack's circle of friends were spellbound and tongue-tied as he spoke. Finally, one ventured, "You are here, standing before us, so you got away somehow! But how did you do it?"

"Fortunately, during my sudden entry into this intrapiscatorial location, I hadn't swallowed my snoose. I know that fish are very sensitive to tobacco, so I mustered what was left of my mouth juices during this frightening situation, and spat a wad right into its esophagus.

"The creature gasped and gagged. Suddenly, its mouth snapped open -- I could see light filtering through the water in front of it -- then, its abdomen contracted and I shot out like a cork on a bottle of my working home brew.

"I zoomed up to the surface, and, believe me, my legs were spinning so fast I actually walked on the water. I reached the shore and continued on into the woods until the lake was lost to my sight. I have never returned to the vicinity of Iliamna Lake. I have no desire to investigate any further the nature of this beast, after my inside view, so to speak."

"I suppose you have some souvenir of this encounter, as you had of the Bigfoot and the prehistoric speakers?"

"I did," said Sourdough Jack. "For years, I had a white streak in my otherwise dark hair, caused by fright, but when my hair turned all white, that memento disappeared. You will have to take my word for this one."

"Oh, we do! We do! No one that we know has had such marvelous adventures in Alaska as you did, Sourdough Jack!" his guests exclaimed, as they took their departures, exhausted by two such exciting tales in one evening.

Romance on the High Seas

Contrary to their usual habit, the residents of
Malamute Heights forsook Sourdough Jack's cabin to
gather at the residence of Captain Frederick Fernando
Stormdecker, known by the nickname of Foghorn, from
his booming voice that was reputed to not only
penetrate but disperse any pea soup type mist.

The Captain had reached an extremely advanced
age and couldn't always manage the hike across the
village from his cabin to Sourdough Jack's place,
because of his aging sea legs. Therefore, his neighbors
frequently dropped in on him, bringing baked and
preserved goods for his larder.

His house fascinated them. It was festooned with
nautical objects -- bits of coral, desiccated starfishes,
nets, ropes, and wooden parts of ships. One might
even say that his house was shipshape, as it resembled
the superstructure of a small ocean-going vessel.

After several months of acquaintanceship with the
old Captain, someone finally asked him why he brought
all those maritime articles so far into the wilderness.

"Perhaps you've heard that old folk tale of the
seaman," he said, "that got so tired of the briny deep
that he went ashore and walked inland with a pair of
oars until he got to a place so far from saltwater that
no one knew what the oars were, and he settled there?
Well, that's nothing but a yarn, because any landlubber
who lived anywhere near a lake or stream would know
what oars are!

"Well, I took all these things, along with a
marlinspike, when I got fed up with life on the sea,
and walked into the wilds of Alaska. When I reached

this place, Malamute Heights, no one recognized what I was carrying, so this is where I dropped my anchor."

"Most seamen retire by the oceanside and can't seem to get enough of that salt air and pounding surf!"

"Well, this old sea dog had just too many close calls and lost too many fine shipmates to want to be reminded of it daily by looking over the sea. I first shipped out as cabin boy on an old windjammer. For years after, I hardly ever set foot on land. During that time, I've sailed the seven seas, rounded the Horn and the Cape, and navigated all the straits from the Straits of Magellan through the Madagascar Straits, to the Bering Straits. I've been in every roaring port that borders salt water. I've shipped on schooners and sloops, dinghies and dhows, tugs and tramp steamers -- you name it, I've been on it. I've faced the raging typhoons of the China Sea, was becalmed for weeks on the glassy Sargasso Sea, and was dang near froze in the Antarctic Ocean. You might think that nothing would astonish me after all this, but I still ran into surprises during my last years at sea."

"Surprises? Would you tell us about one of them?"

"It was in that storm center of the North Pacific -- the Aleutian Islands, where the waters coming north from the Orient clash with the waters moving south from the Bering Sea, causing fogs and rains, winds you can't imagine, and ripsnorting storms that have wrecked many a ship.

"To make our situation even more perilous, I was aboard one of the oldest, most worn-out rust buckets I've ever signed on. Only the barnacles held that old tub together. To add to her miserable appearance, she had been at sea for so long that streamers of seaweed hung down from her hull.

"We were sailing along, on unusually calm seas for this part of the world, when our ship suddenly stopped dead in the water. The engines were pounding away, each beat shaking the old ship from stem to stern, but we were making no headway at all. our navigator checked the tide -- all was normal there. No wind was slowing the vessel. Our charts indicated that the sea under us was free of hidden shoals. We were mystified.

"Then, as if to answer our questions, we saw two long pale rounded objects appear off our bow. They undulated over the surface of the water, then clasped the boat.

"We realized immediately that we were in the grip of a giant squid, a sea animal that has been known to attack even large whales! They are immensely old, and fear nothing.

"We knew also that our vessel, in its worn-out state, could not withstand much manhandling by a sea monster which was so powerful that it could wring our old boat into the shape of a corkscrew!"

"Why didn't you shoot it?"

"We thought of that, but when you are dealing with a creature that might be eighty feet long, it's not that easy to find the vital spot. Besides, in its death throes, it could smash us to oblivion. Our best bet was to try to keep it calm until it got tired of its game.

"As we were sitting there on deck, pondering out this problem, I was suddenly aware of being watched. I looked up, to see that the squid had reared out of the water and was looking over our ship. It peered to the port and the starboard, but seemed puzzled by what it saw. Although we were about on a level with its eye, it didn't seem to notice our presence specifically. It dawned on me that we were in the clutches of a very near-sighted squid.

"Meanwhile, its many arms were waving about over the hull of the boat. Surprisingly enough, its touch was light, almost like caresses. We watched in fascination, almost hypnotized by the gentle movements of its tentacles.

"One of my mates spoke up, 'This devil fish acts like it's in love. It even has a moony look about its eyes!'

"He'd hit it! That squid was acting like a sailor on his first port leave in months. He had taken a shine to our boat. Maybe the strings of seaweed hanging from it gave it a squid-like appearance! Anyway, our near-sighted sea beast was on a love mission, not out for blood.

"But how do you discourage a love-sick squid? How could we get loose of this persistent pest? Knowing nothing about a squid's courtship habits, we figured we might be marooned for a long while.

"About this time, we saw another large form on the horizon. It quickly approached into the range of our binoculars, and we could see that it was another squid under full sail. Evidently, we had blundered into an event rarely witnessed -- the annual migration of the giant Pacific squid.

"It took awhile before our squid detected the arrival of the newcomer. It was getting impatient with the unresponsiveness of our boat, and we were fearful that it might deliver a fatal squeeze. However, when it finally spotted its own kind, it dropped us like a hot Portuguese man-of-war, and splashed after the other sea beast in a happy fashion, leaving us free to continue our voyage.

"The sea has its strange sights, but the night of the pairing of giant squids was one of the strangest for me!" Captain Stormdecker opined. "Even Captain Cousteau hasn't filmed the likes of that!"

The group all agreed that Captain Cousteau and his crew could learn a lot about the giant squid and other mysteries of the sea, by talking to our Captain.

Higher Learning at Malamute Heights

The summer had drawn to a close with one of the largest rhubarb crops in the history of Malamute Heights. The ubiquitous garden pie plant was a marvel to behold, with leaves as large and stems as long and growth as lush as Alaska's other ubiquitous plant, the devil's club.

Being a thrifty lot, the folks there had made rhubarb pies, rhubarb cobblers, rhubarb puddings, rhubarb wine, and all the usual rhubarb recipes, as well as branching out into such flights of fancy as rhubarb au gratin, baked rhubarb Alaska and other innovations.

In the midst of all this emphasis on rhubarb, Ophelia Bumbleforth began to wonder just how this plant species had acquired such an odd, practically un-American name. The other residents, hearing her musing over the subject one day, turned the question over to the one of the few persons in town trained in research. Igor Bivor, the town savant, had spent several years at the University of California, Berkeley. He acquired a bachelor's degree and was well on his way to a master's, when he became embroiled in the rebellious movements of the 1960s. The university administration overlooked his taking part in demonstrations for the free use of shocking and disgusting language, his participation in destroying various college buildings around the country, his campaign to can the chancellor, and his sponsorship of a fund-raising tea for the Symbionese Liberation Army, but decided it was too much when he put Groucho glasses and noses on the statues of the university founders, and he was summarily dismissed from their campus. No longer receiving his educational grants, he was forced to seek a paying job, but found that the business world was less tolerant than the university of his extra-curricular activities. Despite his nonconformist tendencies, he shunned the hippie movement of the times, as he considered his brain his most valuable asset, and wasn't about to addle it with mind-altering drugs. His lack of roots led to his migration to Alaska and his ultimate residence in Malamute Heights, home of the ultra-independents.

After a few days of poring over the many books he had brought into the wilderness with him, he returned to the gathering at Sourdough Jack's cabin.

Donning his glasses, he set up several illustrative posters before the group, and with his best assistant professorial manner, commenced the lecture:

"The name 'rhubarb' is derived from Rhubarbia, the region where this plant was developed." Igor gestured toward a map of northern Africa.

"Today, we shall visit the little nation of Rhubarbia, located on the Rhubarbary coast.

"After decades of being menaced by rhubarbarians, the early settlers of Rhubarbia fenced their boundaries with rhubarbed wire and have been enjoying peace since then. Their industries and services have grown through the centuries. Now, their one town (theirs is a very small principality) is as modern as any of ours. Rhubarbians can get haircuts at the Rhubarber Shop and purchase Rhubarbitol and, if needed, rhubarbituates at the Rhubarbian Drug Store.

"They lead a quiet life, listening to the songs of Rhubarbra Streisand on the radio in the evening, watching "Rhubarbarella" and "Rhubarbarossa" on late night television, and dining at rhubarbecues, while the little girls play with their Rhubarbie dolls.

"To keep healthy, they swim and lift 300-pound rhubarbells.

"Wealthy Rhubarbians often voyage to the Rhubarbados for their vacations.

"Owing to the paucity of information on this obscure but fascinating nation, my lecture will now come to a close."

Expecting applause, Bivor was somewhat dismayed with the groans and negative reviews of his talk. However, having become accustomed to more violent reactions during his previous career as college rebel, he took it all in good spirits, as he knew they would come to him again when they needed answers to hard intellectual questions.

What Next?

Civilization, in the form of electricity, at last reached Malamute Heights, that small outpost in the Alaskan wilderness.

The intrepid pioneers, wearying of lighting their cabins with eulachons (an oily fish, to you cheechakos!) in sconces, finally purchased umpteen miles of wire and strung it themselves from swamp spruce to swamp spruce until it ended up connecting their remote community with a generating plant. The flow of electrons was constant, except when the screaming winds blew down the wires during the winter, or the lines were dragged down to earth by the weight of millions of mosquitos resting their wings by perching on the glistening filaments during the summer.

With the coming of electricity, several of the inhabitants purchased and installed television sets so they would no longer be bypassed by the mainstream of American culture. For those readers who live in America's cities, it may be difficult to realize the excitement of some of these viewers, who, when last exposed to television, had learned their ABCs from Sesame Street, and were now amazed to learn that XYZs had been added to the curriculum.

The American soap opera proved to be the greatest culture shock of all. The audience at Malamute Heights had forgotten that when excitement and suspense reach their highest pitches on a detergent drama, the pace slows to a glacial crawl. Thus, the cronies around the Yukon stove were surprised when they were joined one day by a very agitated Ophelia Bumbleforth, shortly after she had added a television set to her cabin furnishings.

Ophelia was a lady very dedicated to her home life, so she was seldom seen at the gatherings.

"I guess you are astonished to see me," she commented, "but I had to get out of the house for awhile. I've really had a frightful week."

"Whatever happened, Ophelia? We've never seen you in such a state!"

"It's that daytime drama I'm so fond of -- you know, **In the Nick of Time**. It takes so long for something to happen on that program, the suspense has virtually exhausted me.

"Remember how last Friday that nasty estate probater sneaked into Lillian Ida's kitchen during her cocktail party and put truth powder in her flour canister, so she would eat it and reveal her dreadful secret of how she caused her husband to lose his chance for promotion to that job he wanted so much that he'd never forgive her if he found out?"

"Yes, we remember you mentioning something of the sort."

"Well, Monday she started making a pudding, sifting that very flour into the bowl and answering some phone calls meanwhile. Tuesday, she managed to mix in the milk. Wednesday, she added the eggs. Thursday, she put in the cornstarch. And Friday -- "

"She ate it?"

"Oh, no -- she measured and added the vanilla.

"Well, this afternoon, she placed the pan of pudding on the burner and was just about to taste it, when the doorbell rang."

"That was lucky for her! What happened then?"

"She went to the door, opened it, and there stood a young, black-haired stranger. He said, 'How are you, Lillian Ida?'

"She said, 'Who are you? I don't remember seeing you before.'

"He said, 'Why, Lillian Ida, think back to your cousin Patricia, second daughter of your great-uncle Peter, brother to your mother's wealthy father, whom you visited two summers ago.'

"'You mean my dear cousin Patricia in Greenwood, whose son John is married to Fidelia, daughter of Attorney Jonathan Jackson Jefferson, who is facing disbarment from the dishonest conniving of his partner, Anthony Adversary?'

"Well, this talking just went on and on, and I kept worrying about her getting back and tasting that pudding, ingesting the truth powder and thus telling all and losing her happy home."

"We can understand your anxiety. Did she ever get around to eating that pudding?"

"As a matter of fact, by the time that young man finally told her who he was, the pudding was burned and in no shape to be smelled, much less tasted. So she threw it out!"

"That must have been a great relief to you! Actually, you should be relaxed, now that the fatal pudding is gone."

"I was happy -- for two whole minutes. But then that darned Lillian Ida measured out some more flour from that very same canister, and commenced sifting it to begin another pudding, as today's chapter ended! And meanwhile, I'm facing another week of agonizing suspense!"

Sourdough Jack and The Suitor Shooter

Sourdough Jack had been in Alaska for so many years that none of the Yukon stove conversational group knew just what had prompted his journey to this State. No one, of course, was impolite enough to ask why he had come, but they naturally assumed that he had followed the lead of the many early gold seekers. He corrected their impressions with this first exposition of his motives for entering the then Territory of Alaska.

"Many people have wondered why I decided to move to Alaska. This is an extremely personal question, but just to reassure you that I am not one of the 'Ten Most Wanted', I shall consent to tell all at this time.

"During my prime courting years, I was passing through Utah on my way to the Washington clam grounds, when my eye was caught by an uncommonly comely lass. By devious methods, which I won't reveal at present, I gained her friendship. I soon discovered that she was the twenty-third wife of a Mormon (one of the very conservative ones, who refused to follow the rules of monogamy, which was the generally accepted lifestyle, even at that time). Since the government didn't take account of surpluses in those days, she was a pretty lonesome woman.

"As you know from the photographs taken of me at that time, I was a handsome buck myself (somehow those pictures get younger and handsomer every year!), and she was perfectly willing to reduce her status to first wife of me. She had her suitcase all packed and

I was about to skitter off with her, when we were halted in our tracks by a loud 'Halloo!'. Her husband, a suspicious type, stood pointing a gun at me in unfriendly fashion.

"I said, 'Go on! You can't hit anything at that distance!"

"'Maybe so,' he said. 'See that beacon yonder, about three-four miles?' and he aimed that gun, and BLAM -- that light went out like a snuffed candle.

"'What's the range on that thing?' I asked in amazement.

"'Dunno for sure -- maybe 2,000 miles, give or take a few feet.'

"'In that case,' I said, 'won't you give me a ten day running start, seeing you've got all the odds in your favor?'

"'Fair enough,' he said, and set his gun down in a casual manner.

"'Sweetie,' I said, 'I simply have no time for encumbrances right now -- but I'll drop you a postcard from wherever I land!'

"Without further hesitation, I scrunched down on my haunches and took off on a flying gallop due northwest. I was pretty winded by the ninth day, when I crossed the border into Alaska, but I kept running until I reached Nome, just in case that joker had underestimated his range. And, to tell the truth, I liked my new surroundings so well that I've lived here ever since."

Sourdough Jack and the Great Alaska Dog Team Saga

The residents of Malamute Heights had not seen
their friend, Sourdough Jack, out and around for
several days. Fearing that he was ill, they dropped
over to his cabin and found him slouched in his chair,
reading a clipping that had apparently been perused
many times, judging from its worn-out appearance, the
corners of his mouth drooping in a fashion seldom seen
on this jolly old-timer.

"It's this editorial," said Jack. "I got it in the
last mail drop. The author of this is a stranger to me.
However, he claims to have heard accounts of some of
my adventures in the long distant past, and here's
what he had to say about me: 'This so-called
sourdough stretches the truth until a zephyr could
blow his whole tissue of fantasy away like a rotten
spider web. He doesn't know the meaning of veracity.
In other words, he is an over-rated, undereducated,
copper-plated liar!'

"Now, my friends, I ask you, is this fair? Just to
illustrate the type of experiences I have had, I will
relate a personal adventure of mine, never before
heard by man or beast, centered in the slough-bound
interior of Alaska, and let you draw your own
conclusions therefrom.

"In the spring of 1910, I was mushing up from the
Kuskokwim to Fairbanks with my world-acclaimed team
of five malamutes. As the season was drawing near
break up, the trails were poor and several times, the
ice crusts over springs broke with a crash under the
weight of sled and team. I had to neck the sled many
times over bare patches of ground -- that is, get out

there and help to pull it. Finally, we reached the mighty king of Alaskan rivers, the Yukon itself.

"We had ventured out several hundred yards from shore, when I suddenly heard a ripping noise and a thin line of water appeared before my eyes, stretching from bank to bank and lapping at the very edges of the broken ice in front of us. A crashing sound came from behind, and, turning, I saw a similar gap in the ice.

"Then from all four sides and up and down the river came the terrorizing sounds. We were cut off from shore -- drifting on a cake of ice! At any moment that last glass-like haven might break up, too.

"I unharnessed the dogs so they could easily swim away in that event, and tried to figure out a way to get off the ice without falling in the water, as evening was coming on and the nights were still very cold at this time of year. I also didn't want to lose my valuable dog sled, which was loaded with the results of my winter's trapping.

"Despair overcame me, but I hadn't reckoned on the intelligence of my faithful dog team. You know that the Alaskan sled dog has great initiative and has rescued mushers out of some terrible predicaments.

"As soon as my team perceived the situation, they got into a huddle and seemed to be conversing, with many woofs and nods. Then Nakasuk, my wheel dog, went over to the sled and, with his teeth, uncovered a large tank containing refrigerating gas, which I was taking to Fairbanks to refill for a cannery out west. He woofed, and looked expectantly at me. Kikpuk, my leader, dug out the valve and a hose from my baggage. A small amount of gas still remained within the container, and I quickly perceived their intentions. Taking the hint, I assembled the tank and hose, walked to the edge of the ice, and squirted some gas into the water. Immediately, the refrigerating gas froze a yard-square ice cake from the river water. I stepped onto it and squirted gas onto the water two feet beyond the ice square, and it also instantly froze into another small ice cake. In this way, I made a series of steps for the team and me to cross over onto shore. The current of the river was moving about the same speed along its entire breadth and the trail stayed fairly well in line.

"I returned, harnessed the team, and mushed the dogs on ahead, pushing the sled over the ice cakes and lifting it over the watery intervals. In this manner, we safely reached the shores of the Yukon.

"Eventually, we reached Fairbanks, and I related my experience to my club members, who promptly gave silver medals to each member of my dog team.

"If there is even the slightest doubt about this event, a clipping from the 1910 Fairbanks newspaper and a photo of Kikpuk and Nakasuk, wearing their silver medals, should be sufficient to convince the skeptic. As you can readily perceive, that letter I received was indeed grossly exaggerated."

Cornered!

"Of all the creatures in the north," opined Sourdough Jack, during an evening gathering at his rough-hewn cabin, "the most beautiful and dangerous is the polar bear. In the early days of polar exploration, before the advent of airplanes, snowmobiles and automatic guns, this lordly beast had no fear of man. Indeed, he regarded the human as just another source of protein, and would stalk a man in the same fashion as he would pursue a seal or other prey.

"Even at the turn of the century, when I first ventured out into the frozen Arctic desert, the polar bear was feared and respected by the inhabitants of the north."

"What? You were also in the Arctic? We know you have ventured into many remote parts of Alaska, but this is the first I heard about you being in the Arctic!" remarked Naivete Newburg, a young woman who had recently made the long mush into Malamute Heights, in search of the Real Alaska, and found there what she was seeking.

"Yes, I had gone north to watch over a trading post, while the owner went south to visit his long-unseen family. Believe me, I was new to that region, or I wouldn't have found myself in the extremely hazardous situation that I will now relate to you.

"Supplies were getting short on the post, so I thought I would rustle me up a bagful of Arctic hare. As you know, these northern hoppers are the largest hare in the world. A dozen of them would replenish my larder for a week or so.

"I had my trusty shotgun and an old muzzle loader, which I used for larger game, with me, and I soon got my quota of hare and was on my way back to the trading post, when I suddenly spotted or sensed something moving towards me. I peered into the almost blinding whiteness of my surroundings, but at first could discern nothing. Then I noticed some black dots that appeared to be moving. It took me awhile to comprehend that these were the nose and eyes of the Arctic's most feared predator, a giant male polar bear. Circling about like the dreaded great white shark, he had caught my scent and then zeroed in on my trail.

"I knew my shotgun wouldn't have much effect on this animal, who was well protected with his heavy coat of fur and mighty bone structure, so I drew out my ancient but reliable muzzle loader, and started to load it. It was then that I discovered that, in an almost unbelievable bit of carelessness, I had either left my iron ball shots behind or had lost them somehow in the snow. I had my powder and my wadding, but without the shot, I was as helpless as a baby seal in a nest of killer whales.

"Meanwhile, the bear grew closer. He was just a little cautious, because I was an unfamiliar creature to him -- perhaps the first human he had seen, as these bears live a solitary life among the ice floes of the north. I began to shout and wave my arms about, thinking to confuse or unnerve the creature. Instead, he became bolder and picked up his pace, as he sniffed the air and apparently liked what he smelled.

"My feet wanted to run, but my head told me that would only embolden the animal, and I would be no match for it in speed. Meanwhile, it kept looming larger and larger. My adrenalin raced and engendered a constant flow of ideas for my survival in my brain. Unfortunately, none of them was feasible and the mankilling bear was drawing ever nearer.

"Then, it tensed for the charge. I stood up straight, holding my muzzle loader as a club, knowing I was hopelessly outclassed by this powerful bear, but determined not to surrender like a coward. The excitement of the moment caused beads of perspiration to break out on my forehead. When these hit the frigid Arctic atmosphere, they froze into round pieces of ice. Suddenly, a thought came to me. I jammed powder into my muzzle loader, tamped it (while the bear paused in some astonishment, trying to figure out my activities), then stroked my hand across my forehead, gathering the balls of ice which kept forming on my brow. I rammed these down the barrel and packed them tight.

"Meanwhile, the bear's appetite overcame its curiosity and it again crouched to gather speed for the final lunge. With a mighty roar, it left the ground and zoomed for me. I aimed my gun straight at its head and pulled the trigger. The heat of the exploding powder melted the ice balls, and a stream of water emerged from the barrel. It froze on the spot, in the Arctic air, into a large, white, pointed icicle which struck and penetrated the bear's head, just as his shadow loomed over me. With a cry, he fell to the ground, lifeless.

"It took a while to get my nerves under control after this close call. I still couldn't understand why the bear died so quickly. However, some months later, when I was describing my adventure to the trader, who had returned to the North, he came to the conclusion that the intense cold of the icicle had instantly frozen the bear's brain, giving him a quick and painless death.

"If you have any doubts about this incident, you are free to examine my polar bear rug."

Sourdough Jack's neighbors, who knew better by now than to question any of his accounts, examined the huge, snow-white bear hide, and did notice an odd bit of seam work on the head, where the hide had been patched. This at least confirmed that some large and sharp object had indeed entered the head of the bear and caused his demise.

Richard Barry '88

Star Light, Star Bright

It began the same way as any other evening in
Malamute Heights -- the sun went down, everything
got dark, the stars and planets appeared in the sky,
and lights went on in the cabins. Although it was late
fall, the harvest moon hadn't risen, so the firmament
appeared unusually bright.

Igor Bivor was the first to notice that one of the
stars was behaving erratically. It darted back and
forth, spun around a few times, then seemed to get
larger and brighter. He dashed home for his
binoculars, and was startled to see an igloo-shaped
object descending on Malamute Heights.

Fearing some type of meteor fall, he called out
the others from their cabins, and they retreated to the
nearby hillside to observe in wonder.

The flying igloo zoomed down and made a soft
landing in the town field. A voice through a
loudspeaker crackled through the air: "Come down
here! You cannot escape us. Anyway, we do not
intend to harm you."

Hesitatingly, the group returned to the village and
saw a door open on the side of the vehicle. One by
one, the passengers of the strange craft emerged, and
they too looked very strange. They were translucent,
of a milky blue color, and oozed rather than walked
across the ground.

"Who are you? What is the meaning of this?"
asked Sourdough Jack, who was the oldest and figured

he had the least to lose in a confrontation with unknown beings.

"We come from a distant planet. We have been observing you for a long time. We want to know more about you humans," said the largest and most authoritative creature.

"How does he know we're humans?" thought Blodge Bumblefield.

"We know everything! As you can see, we read your thoughts. That's how we know your language. We are telepathic, telescopic, telephonic, televisionary, telethermoscopic, and teleological. No impression, no matter how trivial, escapes our attention."

Igor Bivor quickly tried to erase from his mind his opinion that the visitors looked like a gaggle of upright paramecia.

"Why did you choose to come to us? We're such a remote, insignificant settlement. Why didn't you go to New York or Los Angeles, where there would be so much more to observe?"

"New Yorkers are too excitable. Years ago, we received the telecast of the movie, 'Invasion of the Space Aliens,' just as we were cruising over the Nevada desert, giving the drivers there some conversational topics that lasted for weeks. We got such a laugh out of watching that headlong race to get out of New York. However, we didn't want to deal with such hysterical hotheads, prone to panic. As for Los Angeles, we did tune in on that region for awhile, but concluded that the inhabitants there were not truly representative of the human race.

"In fact, we are looking for a completely unflappable study group, free of the mass herding instincts encountered in over-populated regions, a community of diversified types with mutual interests for survival, a laboratory, so to say, where we can speak, intergalactican to human. That is why we chose your town, Malamute Heights."

"Well, I guess you can fit in here, for a while, anyway. By the way, what do you eat?" The thought arose that sometimes humans are on the menu of space visitors.

"Don't worry about that! We have plenty of supplies, we never eat fellow beings," (the speaker's orifice twisted into a smile) "and, besides, since one of the minutes in our lives equals fifty of your years, we don't require much nourishment. It is our long life span, comparatively speaking, that enables us to travel between galaxies.

"Now, down to business. You don't mind if we inconspicuously follow you about, occasionally asking questions, and gather our notes?"

"Not at all. No one really has taken an interest in us since the last census, when the government sent agents to inquire about our bathroom facilities and other amenities, or when some Alaskan boroughs attempted to annex us for tax purposes. They gave up on that idea, though, when they realized that we'd cost more money than we'd bring in!"

The winter rolled by, as the aliens bustled in and out of their motorized igloo, occasionally chatting with the residents, taking notes and pictures and, in general, maintaining a constant but courteous curiosity concerning the inhabitants of Malamute Heights. One even appeared to have taken an unusual interest in one of the unmarried girls of the town, Phoebe Mae Duseldorf. When the other Heightists observed this, they twitted her a little. She blushed, then said she hadn't ever received such gentlemanly attention from any -- man? -- before, in fact, she was the type of person who was apt to be overlooked or ignored in any social gathering, as she was quiet and shy, rather than exuberant and talkative. For this reason, she appreciated the space visitor's intellectual qualities, and he appreciated hers.

The Heightists observed in wonder and some alarm that this mutual magnetism grew as the weeks went by. Finally, Phoebe Mae announced, all smiles, that she and Perullex, as he was named, were planning a marriage. Others on both sides tried to dissuade them, but their minds were made up. So, towards spring, a beautiful little ceremony was held in the space ship, and a radiant Phoebe Mae and Perullex emerged.

Shortly after, the space visitors finished all the loose ends of their study and prepared their ship for departure. Everyone wondered about Phoebe Mae and Perullex. Finally, Phoebe Mae said she and her husband had decided, although this choice was of extreme pain to them both, that she would remain on earth. Because of her limited life span, Perullex felt she would derive more from a terrestrial habitation. At the moment of departure, he enveloped her briefly in a farewell hug, then both pulled apart bravely and he entered the ship.

Word of this outer space encounter and the accompanying love match reached the outer world via the Snowshoe Wireless, and soon a fleet of specially chartered planes arrived, bringing reporters with requests for interviews for **National Hearsay, Star Snoop**, and other supermarket tabloids, along with huge offers of money. Phoebe Mae turned them down flatly and refused to talk to anyone from outside Malamute Heights.

Some weeks later, the day after the annual mail drop, all the residents of Malamute Heights were closed up in their cabins, reading through their accumulations of mail. Ophelia Bumbleforth was working her way through fifty-two issues of **National Hearsay**, when she came upon an eye-catching headline.

"I MARRIED A SPACE ALIEN!" ATTESTS WOMAN OF REMOTE ALASKAN COMMUNITY.

This was accompanied by a drawing of Phoebe Mae, sitting next to a creature with four heads and ten arms. Ophelia brought it to Phoebe Mae, who read through the article and cried. She said they had made something beautiful into shabby sensationalism.

The folks of Malamute Heights noticed a glow, even a beauty about Phoebe Mae during her marriage and afterwards, that hadn't been previously evident. Perhaps the earlier years of put-downs had hidden these qualities from her friends and even from herself. The young single men of the community perceived this new radiance and, one by one, they went to her, trying to persuade her to annul the wedding with Perullex and marry one of them. She gently but firmly turned them down, saying, "Our marriage may be only a second in the life of my husband, but for me, it will be a lifetime."

On cold, starry nights, the people of Malamute Heights are often seen gazing skyward. They deny that they are idly stargazing. They say they are looking for a far-distant sun in the Milky Way, around which revolves a certain planet bearing intelligent life.

All Things Must Pass

Not too long after the space incident, Malamute Heights, as a community, came to an end.

Some of the inhabitants thought it was getting too civilized, what with such outside interference as television, radio, and more frequent mail flights with curious visitors dropping in after the space visit publicity.

Some others had ceased attending the talks around the Yukon stove, preferring to watch television.

Those families with young children said that, although they personally preferred the wilderness life for themselves, they should not hold back their children from opportunities they might find in a more sophisticated environment.

The final blow that determined the move out occurred the year that the federal debt reached such a high point that the President, the Cabinet, and Congress all agreed that something had to be done. Alaska's small congressional force was informed that it was no longer "what the federal government can do for Alaska" but "what Alaska can do for the federal government." A new election loomed. The Republicans agreed to turn all but the most populated cities and towns into a vast resource and military reserve. The Democrats agreed to turn all but the most populated cities and towns into wilderness preserves, to make up for all the environmental mistakes created during past times in the other states. No matter who won the election, there was no place in the scheme of things for a place like Malamute Heights.

At the present time, Malamute Heights is gone. Only the skeletons of rotted cabins linger on, and these are soon to be removed.

Do not weep for this lost haven. As long as the spirit lives, the place will survive.

Not long after vacating Malamute Heights, Sourdough Jack and several of his neighbors moved into a conglomeration of condominiums located in a lowland outside of Anchorage, obtained by them from the Alaska State Housing Authority, which had a large number of such dwellings on hand at the time. When last heard from, Sourdough Jack had moved a Yukon stove into his condo and had removed the television antenna and cable plug-in from the top of the complex, so his neighbors would be forced to visit again! The sourdough starter is bubbling in his kitchenette and his berry concoction is brewing in the closet.

It appears that the stage is set to resume, despite this urban setting, the Malamute Heights genre of round table discussions!

PART TWO

THE CITY

City Life

The adjustments to the restrictions of urban living were not easy for the hitherto free-living refugees from Malamute Heights. However, they soon began to express their individual preferences. Naturally, they weren't allowed to change the outside appearance of the buildings, but they could give full rein to their personalities within their dwellings. Captain Stormdecker, of course, had brought his nautical paraphernalia along, and soon his condominium took on the appearance of an old waterfront den. Justa Succor covered her walls with examples of original art done by her friends and herself. The Blodge Bumbleforth residence was a model of domesticity, with hand-made rugs, embroidered runners and pillows, shelves filled tidily with colorful jars of preserves, and, in the living room, an artificial fireplace with a revolving plastic cylinder that cast flickering lights upon the walls. Sourdough Jack's decor was simple -- a couple of king-sized bear rugs on the walls, his Yukon stove, an old dog sled leaning in a corner, and numerous relics from his mushing and mining days throughout. Lackoff Forsyte never got around to decorating his place, but was content to live in industrial beige surroundings. At their first condo owners' meeting, they agreed on one major change: They retitled their collective abode **Malamute Estates,** in memory of their old home.

The Dreaded Alaskan Mosquito

It was a warm spring evening, and several of
the Malamute Estates residents had ventured out into
one of the small but cozy Anchorage parks to dine
al fresco. However, as the sun went down and the
breeze quieted, the picnickers were suddenly assailed
by hungry hordes of mosquitos. They packed up
their lunches and returned to the safety of
Sourdough Jack's condo to finish their meal. Some
of the newer Alaskans in the group, awed by the
size of these first mosquitos of the year, asked
Sourdough Jack his opinion of those vicious insects
during the days when he trod the Arctic tundra
without the benefit of repellents, such as are
available today.

"One of the most overdone subjects in northern
mythology," said Sourdough Jack, "is the Alaskan
mosquito. One hears so many stories about its size
and ferocity! Actually, it's the number rather than
the size that is so devastating. They come in
swarms and torment you and every other blood-
bearing creature to a condition close to insanity.

"Worst of all, they have adapted to every
northern condition except the dead of winter. Some
come out of hibernation with the first thaws.
Others like it hot. Some like it wet. Others thrive
on dryness. You can't count on escaping from the
beasts! Only once, however, did I encounter
mosquitos of any notable size.

"I was doing a little prospecting up on the
Chandalar that summer. We'd had more rain than
usual that year and, combined with the long sunny
days of summer in Alaska's Interior, this created a

near-tropical environment in which everything grew lusher and larger than life, so to speak.

"I had heard some rumors concerning a small band of immense mosquitos marauding in the district. Although few in number, they had emptied the land of game and were terrorizing the human inhabitants of the region.

"Ever ready to give a hand to my fellow man, I shouldered my shotgun and fearlessly headed into the center of conflict.

"The high-pitched whine that mosquitos make as they circle their prey gave away their position. In fact, as I neared their territory, I found the noise almost deafening, reminiscent of the aviation sorties I encountered Over There during World War One.

"It's the female mosquito that does the attacking and blood drawing, as most of you know, because she needs the protein to nourish her eggs. I don't want you to accuse me of being a chauvinist, but I must admit that every time I encountered a female mosquito, I gave it a blast with my shotgun. Thanks to my deadly aim, the scene of battle was soon littered with fallen bodies, and by the end of the day, only the drones were left. The male mosquito, as you know, is a harmless vegetarian who does little but eat, fly about, and reproduce the species.

"My dogs had been laid low by a summer flu and I needed a little help to haul logs for my woodpile, which was always a source of concern for me during the summer, as it had to be large enough to last through the long and cold winter.

"I took a few of the fallen feminine warriors and set them up in life-like positions. In the nearby trees, I rigged a large, light fishing net. Soon the males appeared on the scene, looking for their lady loves. As soon as they positioned themselves under the net, I let it drop gently onto them. They struggled awhile, but since the males aren't very aggressive, they soon calmed down and proved quite tractable.

"After I had acquired their trust, I put harnesses onto them and, with a brief bit of training, had them hauling logs to my cabin as I cut the trees down. They worked long and hard all summer, but in the fall, began to lag back. I realized that the cooling weather was causing them to become dormant, so I unhitched them and let them free. I must confess I felt a bit sad doing so, as I had become rather fond of them.

"By this time, my dogs had completely recovered and were able to resume their usual duties in harness.

"The drones disappeared into their winter hiding places. The next year, the mosquitos were normal-sized -- small but numerous and, as usual, bloodthirsty. However, we never again saw the large ones. Since I had shot all of the females, the males were unable to reproduce and this unique species vanished.

"On my wall, you can see one of the beaks from the female mosquitos, saved by me as a souvenir of that unusual summer."

His audience moved to the wall to gaze upon a long, black, jagged sliver that somewhat resembled a saber, and they shuddered, while mentally picturing the mayhem such a weapon could produce in the possession of a voracious, persistent insect such as the mosquito!

An Encounter With Art

The Malamute Estates social group went forth one evening to browse through an exhibition of paintings in the style described as "Absolute and Complete Minimal Art."

Upon their return to Sourdough Jack's centrally-located condo, they broke into a lively discussion of modern art in general and this type of art in particular. A couple of those more avant-garde in taste were enthusiastic about the works. Most of the others expressed opinions ranging from befuddlement to indifference. With the exception of a couple of the pieces, Captain Stormdecker remarked, the canvas could have been put to better use as sails. Even the most conservative agreed that they weren't opposed to modern art in total, as many examples showed imagination and skill. However, they felt that perhaps some artists were having fun at their expense -- they couldn't be **serious** about some of those strange concoctions they put out on public display.

Justa Succor, who practiced art herself, had a wide acquaintanceship with artists of all types. For the edification of the group, she rummaged in her purse and brought forth a newsletter from the creator of the works they had just seen, a young man named Art Humbugger:

A Newspaper published with one purpose: to extol one artist:
ART HUMBUGGER!

ARTIST DEBUTS!

Everyone is invited to a special showing of my latest paintings, which I have been working on for just oodles and oodles of days. These new paintings have been described in AMERICAN PAINT AND BRUSH WIELDERS as outstanding in their insignificance and awesome in their lack of technique.

"These paintings are destined to set the world on fire, or vice versa," said the critic of the NEW YORK UNDERSTATEMENT.

"You will probably never see their like again, as the artist has been urged to leave the planet," opined the EAST COAST CODWRAPPER.

"What this artisan has done with three primary colors, three secondary colors, and a multitude of hues somewhere in between has to be seen to be believed," enthused the BOSTON BAY BEWILDERER.

Don't just take their word for it. Hurry on down to Skid Alley Gallery and see these works of art for yourself. I guarantee that you will be impressed, if not depressed.

BARGAINS GALORE

Buy my paintings now and watch the price go up, as my fame spreads from continent to continent. DON'T DELAY!

Artist Endures Persecution

What do all great artists have in common? They aren't appreciated in their lifetime, that's what. Think of Van Gogh. He had to cut off his ear to get attention. Think of Michelangelo. He had to spend years painting a ceiling before anyone appreciated his work. Think of Rubens. Yes, do think of Rubens. He spent his painting career surrounded by tons of food and plump, glowing women. What's he doing in this discussion? Back to the subject. Add another misunderstood artist to the list--me! Yes, people are still arguing about paying 25 cents for one of my paintings. Don't they realize that after my demise, those paintings will be worth at least twice as much as their original price? Or at least one and one-half times as much. Do not miss out on this once in a lifetime chance to cover your walls with fabulous paintings that are bound to depreciate in time.

ANOTHER REVIEW

The BERKELEY BACKBURNER, official mouthpiece of the California Sanitation Workers' Union, has this to say about my work: "This artist's creations have contributed greatly to our overtime pay by adding to our workload.

BIOGRAPHY OF THE ARTIST

The youthful creator of these works about to be honored by an adoring public was acknowledged to be a genius shortly after his birth, when he grabbed a crayon and decorated the wall next to his crib with an abstract melange of zigzag lines intersected by circles. His astonished mother called in an art expert who happened to be running a cigar store down the block, to get his opinion of her son's first renditions. He declared that the work he beheld made cubism look like old hat, and Pollock could stop dribbling globs of paint on canvas, because a new talent was emerging that would eclipse them all.

The artistic talents of this young colossus were protected from any influences that would tend to limit and cramp his style. He was not allowed to look at any pictures -- either representational or abstract--and his mother, who was also his agent and mentor, refused to allow him to take any art lessons (he was excused from school under special dispensation during any periods of doing or discussing art, including finger painting). Thus, his own unique style was allowed to develop, unhindered by 10,000 years of art evolution, and now flourishes in a category of its own.

The final culmination is his present showing, which the public has been waiting for with bated breath for at least five minutes (how long can one hold one's breath at one time?).

Now is your chance to see what the totally unpolluted mind can create when left to its own devices.

TITLES OF THE PAINTINGS

With unusual solicitude, the artist is listing the titles of the paintings, so the viewer can figure them out (how often have you gone to a showing, to remain in absolute puzzlement as to the nature of the art object being viewed?).

So, here are the artist's own distillations of the profound subject matter found in his works:

#1. Scribble in Pink and Blue (A Memory of Childhood)

#2. Snarl in brown, tan, yellow, and ecru: (Tumbling Tumbleweed)

#3. Circles in mauve and fuschia: (Wine Spill on White Rug)

#4. Zigzag in black and white: (Old TV Test Pattern)

#5. Zigzag in black and yellow: (Half a Lightning Bolt)

#6. White paper, wadded into a ball: (Frustration Personified)

#7. White paper, torn into bits and stamped upon: (Deep, Dark Despair)

#8. Pulverized crayons in Wastebasket: (The End).

New Light on Old News

Igor Bivor, the ex-university student of the Yukon Stove conversational group, acquired a passion for ancient history while re-reading his old textbooks. He sent for, and recently received, some microfilm copies of hitherto undeciphered cuneiform tablets from a college museum. After much tedious study and careful transcription, Igor discovered that he had what may well have been the very first journalistic interview.

Rescued from the obscurity of university archives, this priceless document appears in transcription, as read to the Yukon Stove assemblage:

An Interview with Methuselah on the Occasion of his

960th Birthday

"Good morning, Mr. Methuselah. My, you do look chipper for a young man of 960!"

"Humph, a lot you know how I feel at 960. You haven't had the rheumatism for 876 years!"

"I'm sorry to hear that. Are you doing anything special to celebrate this milestone of your chronology?"

"No, I think not. I just celebrate the centennials and semi-centennials these days. My descendants simply don't have sufficient imagination to find new gifts for my annual birthdays. I mean, what would a man do with 960 neckerchiefs, and all in those outlandish colors? No, this is the most sensible compromise."

"I'll bet you've seen many changes in this old world during your lifetime!"

"To be sure! I'll admit I wasn't too farsighted in those early days or I could have amassed a tidy pile of shekels with what I know now! For instance, I didn't see much in the wheel at first, the silly-looking thing, and now everywhere you look--potter's wheels, chariot wheels, water wheels!"

"How about a little bit on your personal history?"

"Well, as you know, I was married quite awhile before our first child arrived. In fact, I was really getting discouraged when I hit my hundred and eighty-seventh birthday without any sign of an heir. Then, to our delight, little Lamech came wailing into the family bosom.

"I must admit the novelty of children and their manifestations subsequently wore off, after walking the floor periodically with several dozen offspring during the next hundred years.

"Er, excuse me. Martha! Can you please keep those great, great, great, great, great, great, great, great, great grandchildren quiet while I am talking? I'll swear, those children seem to get noisier every generation. Now, when I was a boy -- when I was -- good grief, I can't remember **what** I was like as a boy!"

"Do you have any advice, Mr. Methuselah, for those who wish to emulate your long life?"

"Yes. One word. **Don't**. It's too expensive.

"Too expensive? You seem to be living quite modestly."

"I do of necessity. Why, just to keep from tripping on my beard, I've used up ninety straight razor blades through the years. I've had to buy 1,450 pairs of sandals and 320 robes with sashes and other accessories. To list just a few of my expenditures, I've worn out 720 combs, 222 hairbrushes, and have purchased 7,680 bottles of hair tonic and 378 eye-glasses to date.

"I first retired at age sixty-five, then was forced to seek work again. I've retired at least thirty-two times since then, and each time, my dentures ground away and I had to resume working to buy new sets.

"Another thing, life gets terribly monotonous at times. Every time I do something, it seems as though I've done the very same thing innumerable times in the distant past. And how the time flies! I hardly noticed that last century, it sped by so quickly. I tell you, living 960 years isn't all peaches!

"I'm afraid you'll have to excuse me, young men, while I go out and rustle up a few more shekels. I notice my sandals are wearing thin, and my wife is complaining about the appearance of her robe. Ankle-length robes are passe this century, and she is ashamed to leave the house.

"Why don't you come back in a another century or two, when I'll have the time to discuss this further?"

The ancient document ended at this point, leaving one to wonder about the old man's relationship with his younger kinsman, Noah. As you know, Methuselah was apparently left behind when the Ark sailed, as that was the year of his demise.

Instant Philosophy

Some of the Malamute Estates residents dropped in to Sophia Anna List's unit one morning, to look over her latest interior decorating achievements and enjoy a cup of hot herbal tea at the same time.

While glancing through her glassed cabinet, crowded with mementos from her travels about the country and through several exotic locations throughout the world, where her career as researcher and analyst had led her, they were somewhat surprised to find there a small, ordinary jar, of the kind that holds salves, lotions, and other medical concoctions. The label was no longer legible, so finally one of them asked Sophia just why she had saved this particular object.

"It's a souvenir of my younger days, when I was still attending college. This was my first experience with higher learning and I was absolutely snowed under by the wealth of information at my fingertips. Fascinated as I was, my mind could not absorb it fast enough. I often wished for an easier way to assimilate knowledge than to read, repeat, ponder, memorize, and cram for tests.

"While I wandered one day through that modern marketplace of the city, the corner drugstore, I spotted among the planned confusion of pill bottles, beauty aids, and trace tonics, a neatly drawn sign reading 'FREE! One jar of PLATO, regular 29 cent size.'

"Another marvel of this age, I thought. Plato neatly powdered, jarred, and labeled, and how appropriate that this product was in a drugstore, where youth lived in one hormone cream jar, health in the liquid contents of a large amber bottle, and beauty in any of a vast heap of designer-planned containers!

"Now, one could assay to an intimate knowledge of the Platonic theory by way of a generous application of jarred Plato. The twenty-nine-cent Plato could contain little more than the fundamentals of his philosophy; the medium-sized jar would undoubtedly contain a broader knowledge of his theories and perhaps even his biography; while the Large Economy Size would be a receptacle of all the wisdom of the Greeks, plus a declension of the Greek language. Perhaps future months would feature other Classicists, and maybe even some of the moderns -- distilled Einstein for aspiring scientists, concentrated Mozart for struggling musicians.

"The possibilities of this breakthrough intrigued me so much, I could no longer restrain myself. Seeing several jars of 'PLATO -- free samples,' I rushed to the counter and seized one of these, barely noticing the quizzical glance of the pharmacist as I clutched my treasure. Eagerly, I read the message engraved on the side.

"With a jolt, I returned to the world of hard work, sweat, and tears. PLATO was not at all concerned with 'illusionary reflections of the higher plane of learning' -- its sole function was to anchor sliding, clicking dentures!

"Ah, well," I reflected, in resignation, "in another ten or twenty years, I'll probably be needing this very item."

"Pocketing my free sample of PLATO, I strolled over to the dollar philosophical paperbacks. I kept the jar through the years, as a reminder not to leap to conclusions just because I think something is a good idea!"

New Songs of the Open Road

Summer and the great outdoors usually brings out the poetic tendencies of the most phlegmatic of us. True to form, the Malamute Estates social group felt themselves drifting toward rhyme and rhythm at one of their get-togethers, immediately after the Memorial Day exodus which leaves Anchorage half-depopulated, but crowds every fishing and camping site within a four-hundred mile radius.

Blodge Bumbleforth, battle-scarred returnee from a weekend at the Anchor Point king salmon run, read to the group his inspired offering:

May Twenty-six and Thereafter

Oh, fishies, fishies in the brooks,
Have you ever seen so many hooks?
Rod to rod and creel to creel,
Men angle for their finny meal
At every stream and dampish spot.
What hath Izaak Walton wrought?

Sophia Anna List returned from a round trip drive to Fairbanks, and quoted to the group her impression of a prevalent sight along the way:

Gastronomical Astronomy

Sparkle, sparkle, little star
In the headlights of my car.
Are you foil from candy bar?
Beer can, glass, or pickle jar?
The Litterbug observes no ban.
The whole wide world's his garbage can.

Igor Bivor had similar sentiments, stemming from his drive along the Glenn Highway:

That Outdoor Pest Again

Litterbugs, litterbugs fly away home
Leaving their rubbish wherever they roam.
Why should they clean up their overnight lot?
They won't revisit the same camping spot.
If they should drive back, they'll seek out
        new spaces.
They'd never picnic in **such** filthy places!

Ophelia Bumbleforth submitted her poetic observations, based on an early spring expedition, dipnetting at Portage for the elusive hooligan:

Alaskan Lorelei

Hooligan, hooligan, thy siren call
Lures me onward to my downfall.
No matter how high I wear my boots,
Chest-high waders or waterproof suits,
I always step into the watery floods
Two inches deeper than my rubber duds.

Sourdough Jack finished the poetic session with his viewpoint:

We're Tenting Tonight

Campers, campers, over the highway bound
        Tents in every gravel pit,
        Sleeping bags on the ground!
I found a lovely, lonely camping spot --
        Each weekend I set up my tent
        In a vacant Anchorage lot.

Revolutionary Evolutionary Thoughts

Not too often do the participants in the discussions around the Yukon stove delve into profound scientific beliefs. One evening, though, a slide show presented by Blodge Bumbleforth following a trip to Australia led to a discussion of the unusual animal life found on that continent. This, in turn, led to the remark that biologists consider the monotreme, the egg-laying mammal, as a primitive form of mammal. Sophia Anna List, who had done some thinking both on evolution and women's status in modern society, held everyone's attention for the next few minutes with the following distillation of her viewpoint on those subjects:

"The biologists state that the placental mammals (including us humans) are a step or two up the evolutionary ladder from the monotremes. I'm not going to argue with the natural order of things, as envisioned by the experts, but I think it is fun to consider how life would be under different circumstances.

"Humans in certain situations, especially in these modern times, might find some advantages as monotremes. For example, many young marrieds feel that they cannot afford children in their youthful years, while they may still be acquiring advanced education or working their way up from low-paying jobs to better-paying positions. However, the biological clock poses a problem: they fear that in their wealthier middle years, health difficulties may rule out starting a family. As monotremes, however, they could produce their eggs during their youthful years and keep them in cold storage until their bankrolls permit hatching the youngsters.

"Young marrieds who wish to have children early and to continue their nights out at the same time could hire egg-sitters, another avenue of employment for teenagers. This work wouldn't be too strenuous if the hatching baskets were placed within arms' length of the refrigerator and a TV control.

"Automation would probably enter the picture eventually, with home incubators. Don't you agree that there are many positive aspects about monotremism?"

"I suppose," observed Lackoff Forsyte, "if a monotremic child grew into an anti-social adult, the universal judgment would be: 'I knew he was a bad egg, all along!'"

With that strained pun, the meeting broke up for the evening.

Of Ulus and Oosiks

Every summer, along with the migrating birds, flocks of tourists arrive in Alaska, eager to see and learn all about the Great Land. Although most of the tourists come on their own, some are family members of local residents, coming north to satisfy their curiosity about the Forty-Ninth State and to visit their kin at the same time. Two such out-of-staters descended on Malamute Estates one day -- the parents of Sophia Anna List, making their first trip to Alaska.

Although they were an attractive couple, with their tall straight and vigorous bodies, their smooth, rosy complexions, and their abundant hair, flecked with gray, their straight-laced attitude soon put Sophia's friends in awe.

Sophia Anna List had lived away from home for years, and generally conducted her affairs with assurance and confidence. Only with her parents, who were steadfast Moral Minority members, did she lapse into a more childlike state of choosing her words carefully and avoiding controversial topics. This facet of her personality became obvious when she went out with them on a shopping expedition for Alaskan souvenirs.

Her parents turned thumbs down on any mementos made overseas, no matter how "typically Alaskan" they appeared.

They quickly purchased a number of colorful postcards depicting mountains, town scenes, flowers, moose, and bears.

They found ulus (the Eskimo women's knives) to their liking and bought several for friends back home.

They looked at tee shirts, but balked on taking the one which emphasized that "Women Win the Iditarod", because Mr. List felt that this type of sentiment undermined the American family by putting men in a subordinate status.

Then Papa List spotted a long, gray object made of bone in the midst of some ivory carvings.

"What is the purpose of this?" he asked. "Except for the ivory carvings on the ends, it doesn't look particularly artistic to me."

"That is an oosik, Pa," said Sophia, turning a pale pink.

"An oosik? What is its significance? What is it made of?"

"It's -- well, it comes from a walrus --"

"Oh, a walrus tusk! I thought they were whiter and thicker."

"No, it's not exactly from that end -- you know, walruses are awfully obese and flabby, so when they --"

At that moment, to Sophia's relief, her mother called out, wanting to know the origin of those brownish, rounded, oval objects attached to swizzle sticks, ear drops, and necklaces.

"Those are moose nuggets, Ma," explained Sophia.

"Moose nuggets? I've heard of gold nuggets and copper nuggets, but how do they get nuggets from moose? Are they some sort of mineral deposit, like gallstones?"

"No, not really. In fact, the moose nuggets are obtained from the moose with absolutely no harm to the animal."

"Tell me the background of them!"

"Well, the moose nugget artisans go out into parts of the forest frequented by moose. If they are lucky, they will find piles of moose droppings in good condition -- well-shaped, dry, and separated -- which they take to their workshops, cover with plastic, and fashion into novelty items for tourists."

"Do you mean," said Sophia's mother, with a disgusted look on her face, "I've been handling moose doo-doo?"

"That's it, Ma! That's basically what a moose nugget is."

Just then, Sophia's father rushed up. He had been talking to a sales clerk and had finally learned the original location of the oosik in the walrus. He whispered excitedly to his wife and they both withdrew suddenly from the souvenir shop.

After their two weeks of vacation in Alaska were over, Sophia's parents returned to the airport to fly back south. Sophia later reported to the Malamute Estates group that the visitors seemed somewhat relieved to be returning to the Lower Forty-Eight. What with walrus aids to sex and decorated droppings from moose being displayed in Alaskan shops in a flagrant fashion, for everybody to see, they thought the Last Frontier was still a bit too rugged for them.

And Away We Go!

Malamute Estates was not solely inhabited by former residents of the interior community of Malamute Heights. Some of the owners of the other condominiums were gathered into the fold of the group as time went on, and willingly joined their periodic discussions. One very enthusiastic new member, Senator Constant Blastoff, was also an active member in Alaska's legislature and, as you can imagine, he always contributed a great deal to the talks. If he also aimed to garner additional support for his political aspirations through these social contacts, this was also acceptable to his new friends.

"I think I'll dive into the next race for United States Congressman," stated Senator Blastoff one evening. "I've been in one spot for so long that, much as I like Alaska, I feel that I should avail myself of a junket. Not the pudding, but one of those international jaunts we Congressmen are obliged to take since the United States became part of one big world."

"It certainly is commendable of you to decide to forego the comforts of home in order to further international understanding," observed Blodge Bumbleforth, in admiration.

"It's a small price to pay for the welfare of our country.

"My first action upon being elected will be to relieve unemployment in Alaska. I have a number of relatives and in-laws who have been on the jobless list for weeks and who should make valuable additions to my staff.

"Especially my most recent son-in-law...." His voice trailed off, as he mused contemplatively. "Now, he'd make an excellent publicity agent, with the magnificent job he did in promoting himself to the family bosom.

"My first stop abroad would be to the principality of Monaco. Since one of our own compatriots formerly headed the government there, my omission of a visit would amount to an international insult. Besides, I have some unfinished business there, dating from a previous visit. As you know, I always participate fully in the simple enjoyments of the inhabitants wherever I go, and a certain **chemin de fer**, or 'railroad,' game left me, a person of doubtful gambling abilities, with the distinct sense of having been 'railroaded.'

"Next, I shall charter a cruise ship down the Rhine River. I always avail myself, once I am abroad, of the more leisurely types of transportation, thus giving myself time to absorb the subtleties of grass-roots attitudes.

"I shall make a thorough survey of the wine economy and also revisit the beer cellars of Old Heidelburg, an institution at which I devoted a delightful semester twenty years ago!"

He sighed reminiscently and muffled a "burp."

"My motives of stopping there are, of course, strictly political. I always say one can catch the vanguard of political and social trends among the students and intelligentsia of a country.

"I won't attend too many of those official receptions. There are always interminable speeches of 'Thanks for the loan. It accomplished wonders! But there is still so much to be done that, unless we get more aid, I'm afraid we will have to accept that Russian offer -- the one with all the strings attached!'

"I do intend to partake of those functions featuring Premiers, Presidents, Prime Ministers and Princes. The food and drink, er, I mean, the contacts there are generally of the best grade!"

"I suppose you'll be visiting those trouble spots of Lebanon, Afghanistan, Ethiopia, the Berlin Wall, and the Sudan, to mention a few?"

"Good heavens, no!" exclaimed Blastoff.

"I really would like to," he added, with a tone of deep sincerity and regret. "But I hear that people get shot at frequently in such places -- and I wouldn't want to participate in any foolhardy ventures that might subject my honorable State to the expense of electing a substitute Senator!"

"Senator, all of your motives certainly seem praiseworthy, but really, is this the type of program you would pursue in Congress?"

"Not really! But it's certainly fun to contemplate! Who else could lead such a lively, luxurious life than a playboy millionaire, a large-scale embezzler, or the opportunist breed of Congressman -- and the latter category is easier to attain than the first, and more legal than the second!"

A Bucolic Folk Tale

Ophelia Bumbleforth was fond of reading stories to her children, so they could enjoy these little tales and at the same time acquire a love and appreciation of literature. She frequently shopped for books which contained the type of stories she felt would entertain her youngsters. In a recently-published book, she found a story which had an Alaskan background, and she brought it to a Malamute Estates get-together so her neighbors could voice their opinion of it. She opened the book to a page colorfully adorned with cows and other farm animals, along with their buildings, and, standing in their midst, a proud farmer, hands in his bib overalls pockets. She commenced to read:

"Clever Hansel"

Once on a time, in a far northern place called Alaska, was a farm colony. It was known as The Point MacKenzie Dairy Project. It was very new. The leaders of the State of Alaska had become unhappy, because the earlier farm district, the Matanuska Valley, was being filled with houses. So they started a new dairy project. Among the farmers on this project was one who was very wise. His name was Clever Hansel.

The State of Alaska had furnished land and loans that did not cost much. But it had written on a paper that the farmers would have to have certain work finished by certain dates, or they would be in big money trouble. The state sent inspectors around every so often, to see that the work was done.

One day, the state inspector was due to come. This made Clever Hansel very worried. He had plowed his land

and planted his seeds, but fixing his lands and building his buildings had cost so much money that he hadn't been able to buy any cows. And by this date, he was supposed to have cows on his land.

"What will I do?" he said to his wife. "Without any cows, my loan will be taken away, and we will lose everything!"

Clever Hansel's neighbors, Tom Cropp, Bob Reaper, Glenn Harvester, and Sam Mulcher, were also worried. They too didn't have any cows. Only a few of the farmers there had enough cows.

"What will we do?" they all wondered. They got together to discuss the problem.

A few days later, the state inspector came. He stopped at Clever Hansel's farm, and looked at the buildings, the fields, the farm machinery and -- a fine herd of contented cows. He wrote it all down in his notebook.

Then he went to the farm of Tom Cropp. It too had buildings, fields, and cows. So did most of the other farms he visited. He noted it down carefully in his notebook, and said nice things to them for having fulfilled their duties.

The state was happy, the farmers were happy, the cows were happy.

But how did this miracle happen in such a short time?

The farmers who didn't have cows went to the farmers who did have cows and told them their problem.

"Can we borrow your cows, just for the short time the inspector is looking about?" asked Clever Hansel.

"Yes," said the farmers with cows, as they felt sorry for the others, and didn't want to see them lose their farms.

The cows were put into big trucks and carried from farm to farm, just ahead of the inspector. He had noticed the cows at each farm. What he had not noticed was that they were the **same** cows.

The moral of this tale: Counting Holsteins can lead to udder confusion.

Marooned and Forsaken

Captain Stormdecker, known widely as Foghorn, spent
several restless nights pacing the floor of his dwelling.
His neighbors could hear the steady clomp, clomp of his
shoes as he walked back and forth, to and fro, into the
early morning hours. Finally, a committee called on him to
see if he were having worries or health problems. It
turned out that, sitting in his condo day after day, he had
time to remember adventures out of his remote past, and
he was aching to tell his friends about them, but hadn't
wanted to disturb them by calling them at odd hours at
night, when these thoughts came up.

When they heard this, they assembled the entire
Malamute Estates residency, who packed themselves into
Stormdecker's living room, to listen to his ever-fascinating
tales of his career at sea and ease the old man's mind at
the same time.

"It was back in the days before the international
agreement was passed to protect the fur seals. I was down
in one of the waterfront holes of the Barbary Coast --
Frisco, to you -- drinking my Sarasota Springs water, when
all at once I felt dizzy and passed out. Someone had
slipped me a mickey, I'm sure. I woke up to find myself
below decks on that dreaded sealing ship run under the
iron fist of the Sea Demon himself, "Jolly" Rodger, so
called, not because of any good humor that he had, but
because he had the personality and morals of the worst
pirates that ever roamed the Spanish Main.

"Before I could say a word, he roared, 'I am the law
here. Aboard ship, a captain is the judge, the jury, the
prosecutor, and the executor! Just do what I say and
maybe you'll live to set foot in port again!'

"Well, you can believe that I stepped lively whenever Rodger bellowed a command, which was about every ten minutes. I swabbed the decks, reefed the sails, manned the bilge pumps, cleaned the crow's nest, fetched the salt pork and hardtack, and stood my watch, just as the captain ordered. However, no matter what I did, it never pleased that crabby old mariner. I was either too slow or too fast, too early or too late. If I smiled, he frowned. If I frowned, he scowled and swore at me. I began to fear for my life as the days dragged on and our boat moved relentlessly further into the foggy expanses of the Gulf of Alaska, out where we seldom crossed wakes with another ship.

"I was still a growing young sea pup at the time and, although I had already spent some years at sea, I never had served under a captain so tough and ruthless.

"We sailed out along the Aleutian Islands and pursued the furbearers of the ocean -- the sea otter and an occasional fur seal. Finally, we reached a remote, desolate island, just a jagged rock that thrust itself out of the battering surf and stood cold, bare, and wet in the moisture-laden air.

"Old Jolly smiled for the first time since I'd seen him, but it was an unpleasant smile, as though some dark thought had crossed his mind. 'So you want to get off my fine ship, do you? So you don't care for me as a captain? Well, here's your chance!'

"He forced me into a small boat and rowed me over to the island. I looked in desperation at my shipmates, but they were too cowed to make a move to save me.

"The captain made me clamber out onto the rocks, then he pushed his skiff out and rowed back to the ship. The sails were raised and, as the ship vanished into the fog, I heard the mocking laugh of the captain.

"Now I was alone -- free of the fiendish captain, but left on a desolate rock that didn't offer me even a mussel or a seaweed. I scooped up some rain water to drink, and pondered my fate. I knew there were no islands near enough to swim to, and the water was so cold I could last only a short time, if I did attempt to leave.

"I had sat there for quite awhile when, all at once, the island trembled violently. The water appeared to be much higher up the sides of it than when I first landed. 'Strange,' I thought. To make sure, I made a scratch about a foot above sea level. In a short time, the scratch was under the water.

"I recalled an account I had heard some time before, of the mysterious disappearing island in the Aleutians called Bogoslof. Seamen had reported it appearing above the water and receding back under, often taking different configurations when it rose above the ocean. Old Jolly had left me to face a slow but certain doom on this isolated volcanic peak!

"My fate seemed inevitable. The rocks below me continued to edge down into the sea, and the waters crept closer and closer to my last haven on the topmost boulders. I tried to prepare my mind for the end and to stop seeking ideas on escaping, because there was no escape!

"I closed my eyes, so I did not see a ship approach through the fog. Then, a shout in a strange language echoed across the water. I looked up and beheld a vessel, like none I had ever seen during my many voyages about the world. Before me loomed a large hulk, with tattered sails and creaking masts. Its timbers shook in the breeze. Broken ropes hung from the yard arms.

"The sailors on board looked equally shabby. Their clothes hung from their skeletal bodies, their eyes glittered feverishly in their swarthy faces, their dress seemed oddly old-fashioned.

"However, I wasn't in shape to be picky about my

rescuers. I waved my arms and immediately a small boat set out to bring me aboard.

"On board, I tried to converse with the men, who seemed delighted to have rescued me, but I couldn't understand a word they said. Then, one spoke up in English, and asked who I was and what I was doing on that bewitched island.

"I told them the circumstances of my marooning, and then asked what ship I was on, and where it was heading.

"The man replied that this was a Russian fur trading ship, one owned by the free hunters or **promeshleniki**, a ship that had departed for the islands of the sea otter a few years after Vitus Bering's crew had returned to Kamchatka from these newly-discovered islands.

"'Bering?' I asked blankly. The only Bering I had heard of had sailed 150 years before.

"The English-speaking man said he had been hired to work in Russia and had taken the opportunity to join this crew, in the hope of making a small fortune -- enough to return to his homeland and live comfortably.

"I listened to him intently, although his words didn't seem to make a lot of sense. Perhaps this ship had been drifting at sea for so long that the men aboard had gone somewhat daft, I thought.

"He went on to say that they had gathered quite a large supply of furs, and he, for one, was satisfied and anxious to get back to Asia to sell them.

"However, some of the crew, gloating over the treasures they had accumulated, only got greedy for more. They landed at the Aleutian villages and forced the inhabitants to hunt for them. Finally, when some of the people rebelled, they killed a number of them, to frighten the rest.

"The next time that they put out to sea, the boat seemed to travel under its own will. It put out straight ahead, and no matter how they set the sails or turned the rudder, it continued on its own way. Occasionally, they would see a ship or a spot of land in the distance, but the ship would always turn and take them out of sight.

"They consumed their food and water, but they didn't die! Their clothing and their ship deteriorated, but instead of sinking, their vessel continued its relentless voyage, round and round, through the isolated seas of the North Pacific. They became aware that they were being punished for their evil deeds. Their only hope to escape this perpetual purposeless journey, they finally realized, was to perform an unusual act of charity. However, they were forever at sea and found no chance to help anyone.

"That was why they were so happy to see me, stranded in my pitiful condition on the island of Bogoslof.

"At last, they would find out if this could lift the curse put on them over one hundred years earlier.

"Their ship now began responding to their touch. They lay a course, and soon arrived at one of the larger islands of the Aleutians. They dropped me off at a secluded cove, not too far from a settlement. I waved to them as they pulled away from the shore -- and suddenly -- they weren't to be seen.

"I blinked and rubbed my eyes, but they were gone. I made my way to the village and was soon well enough to hire on one of the fishing schooners that stopped by.

"Now, when I hear someone tell of the Flying Dutchman, I don't dismiss the talk with a shrug, as I would have done in my childhood. I hope instead that the doomed Dutchman can someday find peace, as did the crew on the old Russian hunters' boat."

Plot and Counterplot

Most of the residents of Malamute Estates, having left their rural homes behind, had to be content, when seeking fresh air and sunshine, to lounge on their four- by eight-foot balconies or patios or whatever they chose to call their outdoor living space. However, Blodge Bumbleforth's condo overlooked some undeveloped ground, and, being an avid gardener, he managed to purchase a portion, on which he was able to indulge his horticultural hobby.

A combination of midday warmth and light fall showers inspired the inhabitants of the Estates to converse on the simple joys of watching green things burst into fruit and flower under the guidance of the gardener's tender care.

"Yes, indeed," said Blodge Bumbleforth, "I've always enjoyed plunging my hands into the rich, dark soil, planting the seeds and thinning and weeding the plants until they at last mature. However, with my carefree methods, I never did achieve more than a token crop, so last summer, the family and I decided to apply military strategy and modern scientific attitudes toward our garden, with a view to cutting down the annual food bill."

"I've been curious about the new gardening methods -- they sound so complex and fascinating. Please describe your experience to us!"

"Early last spring, after a careful study of agricultural manuals," recounted Blodge, striking a Churchillian pose, "I began Operation Colossal Crop with a mass mobilization of armored equipment -- rototiller, plow, small tractor, shovel, spade, pick, hoe, trowel and pitchfork. Mounting my tractor, I commenced a thorough barrage of the soil. At the completion of this phase, my ground was well churned, aerated, and pulverized.

"My wife, who is talented at deciphering recipes of all complexities, was placed in charge of chemical warfare. She formulated a mixture of nitrogen, phosphoric oxide and potash, added dashes of sulfates, carbonates and borax, and spread this nutritious mixture over our fifteen- by twenty-foot plot.

"Then I installed the anti-personnel equipment around the battleground -- fence posts, nonclimbable fencing, and, with a deference to more primitive psychological warfare strategy, a scarecrow.

"Next, we conducted an organized implantation of pedigreed seeds and infant plants, which were dusted with anti-damp-off powders and dunked in anti-transplant-shock solutions.

"A subtle propaganda move was our staking of those gorgeous seed-packet pictures at the end of each row -- not only to identify the plants, but also to inspire our efforts by the pictured image of our goal.

"Then ensued a brief cessation of hostilities on both sides, as our seeds pushed up slender stems and the young plants busily accumulated new leaves. Each day, Ophelia and I and the three youngsters went out to the garden to see the amazing progress of our plants and to congratulate ourselves on our decision to employ total gardening.

"Our satisfaction suffered a jolt when one June day we saw several of our little plants lying limp and lifeless on the ground. Some crafty insect night-raiders had nibbled through the young stems.

"After another perusal of manuals, the enemies were identified and the chemical warfare department mixed appropriate potions and descended on the garden rows with

Borgiac precision. In a week, the enemy was completely routed.

"However, just a week later, we noticed our adolescent plants disappearing under a feathery growth of chickweed, horsetails, dandelions, and other alien plant forms. It was clear that, even in this age of mechanized and chemical warfare, the situation required a return to infantry tactics. Armed with trowels, spades, hoes, and fingers, the wife, children, and I conducted a desperate plant-to-plant struggle, pulling the enemy invaders bodily from their entrenchments. Some of our vegetable friends were annihilated in the process, but this days' work was a distinct victory on our side.

"Once again, we retired from an orderly, completely friendly field."

"It sounds as if you had a **harrowing** summer," commented one of Blodge's listeners.

"No puns, please," admonished Blodge. "To continue, this last maneuver occurred in mid-July, time for my three-week vacation. The temperature was reaching new heights, the garden was in glorious condition, so Ophelia, the children, and I drove to a lakeside resort for a wonderful session of fishing, boating, hiking, and wind-surfing.

"We returned, tired but refreshed, and of course I immediately rushed back to check on our garden. Our beautiful plants had vanished under a mass infiltration of weeds and insects."

"I suppose you mobilized your forces again and applied massive retaliation principles to the restoration of your plot!" said Igor.

"To tell the truth, that week, Blodge Junior joined the Little League, Ophelia returned to her usual club meetings, my daughter discovered romantic novels, little Budge took up model planes, and I resumed golf practice.

You might say our forces were dispersed and the enemy remained in control of the field until freeze-up."

"Then, you gained nothing from your efforts?"

"I wouldn't say that. In late August, I harvested the ingredients for one green salad, one Irish stew, one cole slaw, and a ten-pound bag of potatoes."

"If I may presume to inquire, how much did this meal cost you?"

"About $525.50, if one includes the fence."

"Are you at all discouraged with your gardening effort?"

"Yes, somewhat," admitted Blodge. "I think I'd give up gardening if I didn't feel a sense of responsibility toward the slugs, cut worms and aphids -- they've come to look forward to my garden every year!"

"Spoken like a true ecologist!" said one of his guests, as they all sat around, munching carrots from Safeway.

Dreams and Fantasies

Igor Bivor came to Sourdough Jack's condo one morning and asked to use his phone to call over their friends. Jack noticed a drawn look about Igor's normally cheerful face and asked, "What's wrong? Is something troubling you?"

"I had a weirdest dream, which has really affected my mood. I'm hoping to exorcise this disquieting effect by talking it over with my friends!"

In a short time, their neighbors assembled, and all were curious to know what demanded their attention so early in the day.

"I had just finished reading the day's newspapers, which I had saved for evening, since I'd been at work all day," Igor began. "Perhaps some of the news stories affected my mind subconsciously. I went to bed shortly after, and quickly fell into a deep sleep.

"Suddenly, I felt myself leaving the ground and rising into the air -- you know about those dreams where you find yourself gliding above the ground? Without any effort on my part, I was soon high among the clouds, looking down at rivers, valleys, forests, and small hills, like the view of a relief map, while to my right and left rose mountains.

"These mountains were remarkably like the Chugach Mountains in appearance, but I did not see the streets, business buildings, and residential areas of our sprawling, vigorous city of Anchorage. Instead, I could see only large trees and dense brush below, with some shells of buildings among them, which looked like ruins of a city and, astonishingly enough, some cleared spaces that bore resemblance to lakeside resorts and golf courses below, and, on the mountains, bared portions suggestive of ski runs.

"I swept lower for a closer look at these oases in the forest, and, sure enough, there were very palatial buildings erected alongside the lakes we know as Goose Lake, Sand Lake, and the other bodies of water we know so well. I saw people relaxing by swimming pools, hiking through the nearby forest, and pursuing their elusive golf balls across lush, well-groomed greens.

"For some reason, I didn't want to make my presence known to these people, so I alit in a tangled mass of forest, a considerable distance from the clearings. When I looked about me, I discovered that I was surrounded by ruined buildings, concealed by the almost jungle-like growth from my sight as I had flown over. The remains of walls, lamp posts, and what appeared to be sidewalks still were discernible. What once were paved streets were cracked expanses of black coating, broken by burgeoning trees and plants, growing haphazardly.

"The scene seemed familiar but strange at the same time, as I walked about, puzzling over these structures. Birds and insects flew about, but otherwise the scene was quiet, basking under a warm sun. I wondered if this was the result of some atomic war, or the consequences of the greenhouse effect -- but how would these explain the inhabited vacation spots scattered throughout this otherwise wasted land?

"I walked along the banks of a stream that resembled Ship Creek, then headed inland, into what appeared to be the heart of the ruins. Finally, I reached a building which was still intact, though with a look of long neglect.

"Cautiously, I opened the large door and entered. The building had large windows in front but the interior was in shadows because of the trees. On the walls were squares like paintings, but they were dark and nothing could be distinguished on them. In cabinets were curious objects, intact but obscured by dust. Finally, in niches stood human-like figures.

"I approached one of them. It was clad in a partly-disintegrated plaid shirt and heavy canvas trousers. I reached out to touch the figure, then drew back suddenly when I noticed that its face resembled yours, Sourdough Jack.

"'What is this?' I thought. 'A mummy, a display dummy, or some kind of wax work?'

"I was too shocked to examine it more closely. Then I saw a placard nearby, of the type used by museums to explain an exhibit.

"I bent over, wiped off the dust, and read: 'The Last Miner.' Beneath it was a finely-printed paragraph describing the life and activities of the typical Alaskan gold prospector and miner, and his relationship to the exploration and development of Alaska. It also explained that the miner and his works had no place in the new order of affairs in Alaska. However, as a reminder of his past associations in Alaska history, this exhibit was erected.

"I moved over to another figure, which, strangely enough, resembled you, Captain Stormdecker. It's eerie how familiar things merge with the supernatural in dreams! Anyway, I turned to the placard and read, 'The Last Fisherman.' This told of the activities so familiar to us -- seining, trolling, bringing the fish out of the sea and preserving them -- a history so closely tied to Alaska that it began soon after the purchase from Russia. But why was he the last fisherman? I read further and discovered that the increasingly technical efficiency of all the world's fisheries, plus the greed that refused to acknowledge limits and territories had cut the fish population to such an extent that the Alaskan fishermen were forced by law to desist and to find other work, to avoid antagonizing other nations to which the United States owed money.

"Elsewhere in the large showroom, I saw monuments to 'The Last Logger,' 'The Last Homesteader,' 'The Last

Farmer,' 'The Last Whaler,' and 'The Last Oil Driller,' among others.

"I moved back near the entrance and noticed a darkened bronze plaque there. On it was engraved, 'A Museum of Alaska's Past - Erected 2005.'

"I was astounded. Somehow, I had emerged into an unknown future age. But what had happened to the city?

"I noticed letters carved over some of the museum doorways, so I looked about until I found a doorway designated 'Archives.' I went in, and found books and papers on the shelves. Most of the pages were brittle, stained and unreadable, but I found a book entitled **Alaska's History,** which was of obviously superior quality, as its pages had survived the years of neglect. I brought it over by the window and glanced through it, lingering over the passages which explained the changes that had led to the scene before my eyes.

"In brief, I read that the people of the United States had become alarmed over the prospect of industrial activities moving into the largely undeveloped government lands of Alaska, and, urged on by powerful environmental lobbyists, had made national parks out of vast tracts of lands. Human activities in these lands were restricted more and more over the years. Finally, the parklands were declared 'primitive' and no one but government personnel were allowed to enter.

"Then, it appeared that activities in the regions surrounding the parks affected the ecology of the animals and plants within, so these were turned by law into additional preserves.

"Meanwhile, the oil output had diminished, and energy sources of other types were developed throughout the nation. The revenues for the state and residents based on oil extraction fell to a point that the economy was demoralized. Mining, fishing and other resource use had been abolished and no manufacturing or other sustaining activity had been encouraged to develop. The state, city, and town governments, which had become ossified into patterns of spending to reward their friends and backers, were unable to adjust and finally disintegrated.

"Finally, the population fell to such a low point that the remaining few were prevailed upon to leave, so that the entire state could be converted into preserve.

"At first, it was desired that no one but guardians of the land would be allowed to remain. This museum was erected as a reminder of Alaska's previous history, for the edification of the preserve personnel and the occasional Congressional visitor.

"However, as time passed, the keepers of the budget in Washington, D.C. began to rebel at the cost of sustaining a primitive wilderness preserve. They decided to set up luxury resorts in selected parts of Alaska, for the use of wealthy people who could pay the price for a vacation in exclusive surroundings.

"The history ended there, so I pieced in the subsequent developments.

"The visitors must have had little or no interest in the city that existed there, so it had been abandoned, to be gradually reconverted into forest.

"Saddened by the changes about me, I once again rose into the sky and wheeled about, to leave the land as quickly as possible. I woke up suddenly, startled to find myself in my bed, with the noise of the city outside my window! However, I just can't seem to shake the odd feelings that linger after this dream!"

"Relax! Forget it!" urged his friends. "You simply had a very confused nightmare. It could never happen!"

"You're right," agreed Igor. "It could **never** happen!"

The Leave-taking

As the sun slowly slips behind Mt. Susitna, turning the slate gray waters of Turnagain Arm into a riot of crimson and gold, we will bid farewell to the tenants of Malamute Estates, leaving them to continue their discussions on diversified and sundry topics without our intrusion!

Perhaps one of the gang will again choose to record more of their tales in the future.

Until then, au revoir, auf wiedersehen, ciao, and:

havva nice day!

GLOSSARY

Cheechako:

A person who had not enjoyed the opportunity of living for any length of time in the Great State of Alaska.

Sourdough (noun):

One of the fortunate few who have lived in Alaska for eons. Some say the word is derived from the person being "sour" on Alaska but without enough "dough" to get out. Sourdough Jack denies this vehemently.

Sourdough (adjective):

Sourdough starter: a bubbling mass often found in a draft-free corner in the cabin. Used to make sourdough bread and sourdough pancakes.

Home Brew:

Another bubbling mass found in corners of some people's cabins.

Hooligan or Eulachon:

An oily, edible fish resembling a smelt. Also called candlefish, as they were used to light houses in primitive times, when one didn't mind a little fish smell in the dwellings.

Snoose:	A chewing tobacco concoction, often sold under a Scandinavian trade name. Not recommended by the Surgeon General of the United States nor anyone else.
Snowshoe Wireless:	Or Mukluk Telegraph. That indefinable Alaskan ability to transmit verbal news in a wide circular wave, across mountains, ice fields, and broad barren expanses, by no visible physical means.

Time to 'Fess Up!

The compiler of these backwoods sagas, who finally consented to be named, after being reassured that the inhabitants of the former Malamutes Heights would not hold any grudges concerning the revelation of their conversations and that the public in general wouldn't believe a word of them, anyway, is revealed to be Mary J. Barry, aided by her sons, Richard and Ronald. Richard contributed the drawings, and both added ideas to some of the stories.

Three of these accounts were based on much briefer tall tales heard by the author during her school days in Seward, Alaska, way back when. The tale about the Sourdough and the Mormon was related by Pack Olson, that of the bear and beavers by "Boots" Anderson (who didn't reveal how he escaped, either), and the encounter with the polar bear by the father of a school friend. The author and her assistants must take the blame for the rest! There really was a dental adhesive on the market, called PLATO. The story about the migrating Point MacKenzie cows is true.

Finally, the tales were written in fun. We longtime Alaskans enjoy our myths, traditions, and points of view, and we hope the reader accepts them in the same spirit.

OTHER BOOKS BY MARY J. BARRY

OUT OF PRINT:

The History of Mining on the Kenai Peninsula
(to be reprinted)

The First Twenty-Five Years of the Cook Inlet Historical Society, 1955 - 1980

IN PRINT:

Seward, Alaska: The History of the Gateway City, Volume I, Prehistory to 1914

The first of two volumes. A detailed account of this   Alaskan coastal city, including the prehistoric and Russian periods, its founding in 1903, and events in its development to 1914. $25.00.

The Samovar, Its History and Use

A booklet concerning the ornamental Russian tea urn, part of the household scene in Alaska during the Russian period. $4.00.

Available in several Alaskan book stores and gift shops, or by mail from:

M J P BARRY
323 West Harvard Ave.
Anchorage, Alaska 99501

If ordering by mail, please add $2.00 postage and packaging for SEWARD, ALASKA and $1.25 for THE SAMOVAR.